"INDIANS," JOSH SCREAMED. "HEAD FOR THE FORT."

He kicked Rambo in the sides, so hard the horse almost shot out from under him. I kicked Beauty too.

The cows raced ahead of us. They had their tails up. We waved our arms, yelling and hollering as we chased them across the top of the hill and to the safety of the blackjack fort ahead of us.

Right as we topped the hill, Beauty stumbled. She didn't go down, but we were running so fast when she tripped, I almost fell out of the saddle. I grabbed the horn and slipped over to the side. I had to fight to get myself back up.

Beauty could run like the wind! It wasn't until after the cows had disappeared into the safety of the blackjack trees and we turned and started walking toward home that I noticed Beauty limping. . . .

BEAUTY

BY *Bill Wallace*

SCHOLASTIC INC.
New York Toronto London Auckland Sydney
Mexico City New Delhi Hong Kong Buenos Aires

This book is a work of fiction. Any references to historical events, real people, or real locales are used fictitiously. Other names, characters, places, and incidents are products of the author's imagination, and any resemblance to actual events or locales or persons, living or dead, is entirely coincidental.

ISBN-13: 978-0-545-09785-7
ISBN-10: 0-545-09785-1

Published by Scholastic Inc., 557 Broadway, New York, NY 10012, by arrangement with Aladdin Paperbacks, an imprint of Simon & Schuster Children's Publishing Division.

12 11 10 9 8 7 6 5 4 10 11 12 13/0

Printed in the U.S.A. 40

First Scholastic printing, September 2008

To Carol, with love

BEAUTY

CHAPTER 1

Sometimes you remember dreams. Sometimes you don't.

When the sunlight came popping into my bedroom early that morning, I remembered dreaming about Daddy and the Morning Trail.

It was in July that we went. We'd pack the tent and head off for the mountains. We always traveled the old highway that took us to Colorado Springs, then wound around through the mountains and up over Independence Pass.

Lost Man Camp is where we usually stayed. It was right over the Divide—up really high. Sometimes when it was full, we'd have to stay at one of the lower campgrounds, but mostly it was Lost Man where we stayed. The air was clean, and it was quiet.

Daddy would pitch the tent, and I'd put out the sleeping bags and get the camp all neat and set up while he cooked hamburgers for supper. In the morning we would catch trout in the small pond about a quarter mile above the camp. He'd cook them for breakfast, and then we'd drive down through Aspen to where the High Mountain Corral was.

Daddy would rent horses, and the guide would take us and a bunch of other people up to Maroon Bells on the Morning Trail. We loved riding horses. Daddy liked to go right after breakfast. He said it was the prettiest time of day, the time when the world was waking up after a good night's sleep and everything was fresh and crisp and new.

Now it was July. Thinking of that and remembering Lost Man Camp and the Morning Trail brought a smile to my sleepy face. I kicked the sheet back and sat up.

I had to blink a couple of times to get the sleepy grit out of my eyes. When I looked around, I felt my shoulders sag, felt the sigh whoosh from my chest.

I wasn't home. I wasn't in my room at our apartment in Denver. I was at Grampa's house.

When I looked out the window, I couldn't see the Rocky Mountains in the west. All I could see were rolling hills and brown wheat and endless clumps of red Oklahoma dirt.

Everything was unfamiliar, and even in the cool of the early morning it felt hot and humid and dusty.

I gave a little groan, then flopped back down on the bed. I grabbed the pillow and pulled it over my face to shut out the light.

I was remembering that almost two years ago Daddy left—in fact, longer than two years ago. I remembered Mama and Daddy fighting a lot, yelling at each other, Daddy storming out of the house, Mama crying.

Lots of kids in my school came from families who had split up. But that was always something that happened to somebody else's family, *not mine*. Mama and Daddy kept telling me that. I'd hear them yelling at each other late at night. Most times it woke me up, and I'd go plopping barefoot into their room to see what was wrong. They'd let me sit on the bed with them. They'd say they were just having a "discussion" and that everything would be all right.

But when I went back to my room, I'd hear them start up again, just as soon as they thought I'd fallen asleep. Either that, or the next night the fighting would wake me once more.

Then the year I started fourth grade Daddy took

his clothes and everything and moved. He and Mama were getting divorced. He told me he still loved me very, *very* much but that he and my mom just couldn't get along together anymore. He said that even though he was leaving I was still his son. He'd see me every time he could. He'd even take me to Lost Man come summer.

Summer came.

Daddy didn't.

Mama and I made out pretty well on our own. Lots of times I'd hear her crying herself to sleep.

Lots of times I cried myself to sleep, too, but when you're eleven and might-near grown, you don't let anybody else hear.

I helped with the housework—did the dishes and swept and took the trash out. Mama worked at the AT&T plant in Denver. We didn't have much money, and we couldn't do a lot of stuff like go to the show or go over to Elitches Amusement Park and spend time on the rides, but we did all right.

Then a little after Christmas the plant had a big "lay-off." I didn't know what that meant. Mama told me it was when there were more people working than the plant could afford, so some of them had to be let go. Since Mama had only been working about a year and a half, she was one of the first.

Things really got tough then. Mama couldn't find

another job. She really tried, too. Before long, we got behind on the rent and the phone bill and the electric bill, and after about two months Mama had to sell the car to pay all our bills. Then there was no way for her to get to and from work even if she could find a job.

Daddy said he'd send us some money to help out, only he never did.

"Your grampa's been wanting us to come see him for a long time," Mama told me one night. "I called him on the pay phone downstairs just a while ago. He wants us to come live with him."

Mama put her hands on my shoulders so she could look me straight in the eye.

"Your grampa's old and cranky and set in his ways," she said. "It won't be easy for either one of us. But I don't know what else to do. We're out of money. Just barely enough for bus tickets, and if we buy the tickets, we won't have enough to buy food. Won't even be able to eat till we get to Oklahoma, but . . . It won't be for long. Things are supposed to be worse in Oklahoma than they are here, but they say the price of oil is going up and that will mean more jobs. Grampa wants to help us till we get on our feet again. Okay?"

"Okay."

Mama gave a big long sigh. "I don't know if you'll like Oklahoma. I don't know if you'll like Grampa. He takes a lot of getting used to. But, well . . ."

I remembered smiling and touching Mama on the cheek. "It's okay. I'll like Oklahoma and I'll like Grampa."

I lifted the pillow off my face and sat up in bed again.

I felt the warm, sticky breath of the Oklahoma wind on my face.

"I hate Oklahoma," I muttered. "I'm not too crazy about Grampa, either."

"Luke!"

I jumped. Then there was a loud *bang, bang, bang!* on my bedroom door. That made me jump again.

"Breakfast." Grampa's gruff, gravelly voice sounded from the other side of the door. I'd only been here three mornings, but I knew that was the only call I'd get.

The first morning, I got up when that loud pounding shook me from a good night's sleep. I went dragging into the kitchen in my pajamas. I found out really quick that you got dressed before you came to Grampa's table. The second morning, I was so darned sleepy I pulled the pillow over my head and dozed off again. I only slept for a few minutes, but when I got dressed and came in to eat, Grampa was helping

Mama stack the dishes. I started to say something, but Mama shushed me. After Grampa went outside, she explained that Grampa had a rule that you came to breakfast when you were called or you didn't eat. She said she'd tried to save me something, but he dumped the stuff out before she could get to it.

It made me mad, but there wasn't much I could do about it, and being mad didn't help either. So I guess I got over it pretty quick.

I didn't much like being bossed around. When Daddy left, Mama let me do things pretty much my own way. She didn't gripe and fuss and correct me all the time.

I'll show Grampa, I thought. I'll just lay here and not even go in for breakfast.

Then the smell of that fried bacon got to me.

"Morning," Mama greeted with a smile.

I smiled back and finished buttoning my shirt.

She held an egg up. "One or two?"

"Two," I said, yawning. I plopped down on my chair. No sooner had my bottom hit the cushion than Grampa growled, "Get the orange juice out of the ice box. Glasses are in the cabinet left of the sink."

My lip curled as I glared at the back of his head. You could at least ask, instead of ordering, I thought to myself. But I didn't say anything.

He was standing near Mama, pouring himself a cup of coffee. For a second I thought about sticking my tongue out. But the way things had been going, I'd probably get caught, so I just got up and fixed the orange juice like he said.

Mama sure knows how to fix a good breakfast. Nobody talked much. We just gobbled down the bacon and the scrambled eggs and the toast with grape jelly.

"Figure it's time we put you on a horse," Grampa growled as he stuck another pile of scrambled eggs in his mouth. "I can always use help moving the cattle. Figure it's time you started earning your keep."

"A horse!" The bacon I was chewing almost fell out of my mouth. I had to reach up and poke it back in. "You mean you got a horse? A real honest-to-goodness—"

"Don't talk with your mouth full," Mama cut me off.

I started to ask why Grampa could talk with a mouthful of eggs, while I couldn't talk with bacon in my mouth, but I decided it was best to just shut up and keep chewing.

"Yep," Grampa answered me. Then, when he finished chewing his eggs, he added, "A real honest-to-goodness horse."

My throat made a loud gulping sound when I swallowed the last of my bacon. "Where? When?"

"Got up early this morning and went over to Mike's. Figured if I—"

"Who's Mike?" Mama interrupted.

Grampa motioned with his thumb toward the kitchen window. "Mike Garrison. Bought the old Sampson place about six years back. Moved in and made a right nice horse ranch out of it. Nice fella. You'll have to meet him sometime."

My eyes were getting big. "What kind of horse did you get, Grampa?"

Mama put her empty orange juice glass down. "I didn't know the Sampsons had moved. I figured they'd stay on that ranch till their dying days."

Grampa shrugged. "I figured they would, too. About five years back his health started giving him problems. Then an oil company drilled a well on the northeast corner of his section. It was a good one, and the oil prices were up back then. Anyhow, they figured with his health being so poor, they couldn't run the ranch. With the oil well giving 'em all the money they could ever want, they just up and moved to a big house in Chickasha."

I tugged on Grampa's sleeve. "What kind of horse?"

"Are Mary Ruth and her husband still in Chickasha?" Mama asked.

"Yeah. The Sampsons moved in right next door to

Mary Ruth. That way they get to see their daughter and the grandkids any time they want. Got a real pretty home. We'll have to drive by next time we're in town. They got this brick fence about eight feet high around the whole place and—"

"The horse, Grampa!"

For the third time both of them just totally ignored me.

I couldn't believe it. Here Grampa had brought a horse home, just for me, and I couldn't find out a darned thing about it. Every time I asked, they kept talking about old times and the Sampsons (who I didn't even know) and about who'd moved where and who still lived where and what happened to old So-and-So, and who died while Mama was away and who was still living and who got sent to jail and who got married and who got divorced and . . .

I couldn't believe it! It was enough to make me want to scream! But all *that* would do would get me yelled at, so I didn't. Instead, I got up from the table.

If they wouldn't tell me about the horse, I'd just go out and see it for myself.

"Where you headed?" Grampa asked.

I bit my bottom lip to keep from yelling. "See the horse."

"After you do the dishes."

My eyes rolled clear back in my head. Then, the

second Grampa told me I had to wash the dishes, he and Mama went right back to talking.

I've never done dishes so hard and so fast in my whole life. Most of the time I was scrubbing and washing away, ignoring what they were talking about. But sometime after they'd been talking for about ten or fifteen minutes, I heard Mama ask about the horse.

I felt my ears perk up.

"Beauty," Grampa answered.

"The old mare I used to ride?" Mama yelped.

"Same old gal." I thought I heard Grampa almost chuckle.

"I can't believe it." Mama shook her head. "I haven't thought about old Beauty for years. I figured she was long dead."

"Nope. Still going strong." Grampa scooted back from the table. He fished his crusty old black pipe out of his pocket. "Mike's been using her as a lead horse for some of the colts he's breaking. I told him about Luke needing a horse to ride, and then I went straight and got her. Even gave her a bath. Looks might-near as white and shiny as that year you rode her in the rodeo parade. Remember?"

Mama nodded. "I'll go out with you. I haven't seen her in years. Just let me finish my coffee and—oh, shoot! That Mr. McPhearson's supposed to call about the job at the belt factory. I want to see Beauty again so bad, but I better wait here. He's supposed to call about nine."

I snatched Grampa's coffee cup and dishes out from in front of him. Mama still had hold of her cup, so I left it. But in a second or two the dishes were finished, and I was ready to go.

I just *had* to see this new horse Grampa brought. I could almost picture her in my mind. All white and shiny, glistening in the bright sun.

And with a name like Beauty. . .

CHAPTER 2

It wasn't the Morning Trail, but I was riding.

Well, not really riding. Grampa was leading Beauty around with me on her back, like I was some little kid on a pony ride at a carnival. But at least I was sitting on a horse again.

She looked kind of old and ragged when I first saw her in the corral. But from up here on her back, she was *beautiful.* Her mane draped to the right side of her neck, fine and smooth as corn silk, like the touch of butterfly wings against my hand as I held the reins low in front of the saddle.

While Grandpa led her around the pen, I couldn't help noticing how her walk was as smooth and gentle as a snow skier gliding down fresh powder. Still, I could feel her power and strength.

Grampa led her slow and easy. About all I could see of him was his white hair. Every now and then a puff of smoke came curling up over his head and back toward me. It smelled like a mixture of coconut and old dirty socks, kind of good and kind of yucky, both at the same time. I sure hoped Grampa's pipe tasted better than it smelled.

"Got five acres in this pen," he said over his shoulder. "Think I'll just have you walk her in here today. Let you two get used to one another 'fore I turn you out on your own."

I slumped a little in the saddle. "I know how to ride, Grampa," I said, feeling a little disgusted. "I've been riding with Daddy up in Aspen for years."

A big puff of smoke rolled back over his head. He stopped and turned to me.

"It's like trading in a bicycle for a motorcycle," he said, smiling.

I felt a frown tug at the corners of my mouth. "Huh?"

"Beauty. Even though she's old, she still ain't exactly what you're used to."

The corners of my mouth dropped farther, since I didn't have the slightest idea what he was talking about.

"What do you mean?"

"Beauty, here." Grampa patted the horse on the side of her neck. "She ain't like the horses you're used to." He cocked one burly, rumpled eyebrow at me. "Your mom's written me a couple of times 'bout you and your dad riding up in the mountains. You rode stable horses or trail horses, didn't you?"

I shrugged.

Grampa grinned. "Well, trail horses are used to following another horse. They keep their place in line and track their back feet." He stopped, noticing the puzzled look on my face. "'Track their back feet' means they put their back foot down in the exact same spot where their front foot just left. Makes for a good sure-footed mount. Good for riding narrow mountain trails."

He took another puff on his crusty-looking black pipe.

"Anyhow, a trail horse is good for following. They don't stumble much. Best horse there is for being in the mountains. But if you ever tried to make one gallop, you'd beat the leather off the heels of your boot and still wouldn't be able to get it into a trot. Right?"

I felt my lip curl, remembering. "I guess."

"Little ole mare you're sittin' on ain't no trail horse. You kick her like you have to do one of them, she'll shoot clean out from under you. Leave nothin' between your butt and the ground but empty air. Got a lot of get-up-and-go. Gonna have to take it easy with her till you get used to the way she handles."

I tried to smile, not really enjoying this long-winded lecture.

"Mike Garrison took her on the rodeo circuit five, no, six years back. Used her for a roping horse and trained her for cuttin', too. You get yankin' the reins, she'll move on you, and you won't know where she went till you scrape the dust out of your eyes and look around from where you're sittin' on the ground."

I smiled and nodded my head at Grampa. I heard his words, but I really wasn't listening to what he said. Shoot! Daddy had been taking me riding since I was five.

"Can I ride now?" I tried not to sound too disgusted.

Grampa's pipe had gone out. He looked down and stuck his finger in the bowl to pack the ash. I waited for more advice while he lit his pipe again.

I couldn't help noticing the funny, knowing smile on his face when he motioned to the far end of the five-acre pasture.

"Go right ahead."

He let go of the reins and stepped back.

I remember thinking to myself, I'll show him who knows how to ride.

And I remember pulling the reins.

And I remember kicking Beauty in the sides with both heels.

But that's about all I remember.

The next thing I knew, the right side of my bottom hurt. My head was aching and throbbing something terrible, and Grampa was picking me up out of that red Oklahoma dust. He snatched me off the ground like I was no heavier than a sack of feed and pitched me back on the horse. It all happened so fast, I hardly knew I'd been thrown off, except for having a sore tail and a terrible headache.

Grampa stuffed his pipe in his pocket and kind of growled as he cleared his throat.

"Now that we got your attention, you figure I need to talk to you again or can you remember what I said?"

I blinked a couple of times, trying to make sure where I was.

"I can remember." I picked some sand out of my teeth with the tip of my tongue.

Grampa backed off again. "Some people got to do everything the hard way," he said with a shrug.

This time I latched onto the saddle horn. I'd take it a little easier. It'd been a long time since Daddy and I rode in Aspen. I just needed to get used to the horse, get used to riding again.

Easy as could be, I brushed my heels against

Beauty's side. She leaped into a gallop that sent me sliding against the back of the saddle. I yanked on the reins. She stopped so quickly, she almost threw me over the saddle horn and onto her neck.

Behind me I could hear Grampa chuckle. It made me so mad, I wished I had something to throw at him.

"Just use your knees," he called. "Don't kick—just squeeze with your knees when you want her to go."

Beauty and I sat there for a long time. Finally, I got up the nerve to try and make her move. I held the reins really tight and squeezed just a little with my knees. It worked. She started walking.

Still, I was scared and tense and shaking so much I could hardly enjoy riding. We walked around the pen a couple of times. Then, feeling a little better about the whole thing, I squeezed a little more with my knees.

She started trotting.

Now you're getting it, I told myself. Now you can handle her. You're riding her now.

And as I trotted past Grampa, I turned to smile at him.

This time I landed on my right shoulder. Stars popped in my eyes for a second. I hurt something terrible.

When I finally managed to sit up, the old horse was

standing a few feet away, staring at me with a funny look on her face as if to say: "Well, what are you doing down there, stupid?"

Her standing and looking at me almost made me madder than getting thrown off. The first time, I guess I asked for it—trying to show off to Grampa and prove what a good rider I was. But this time . . .

I was on my feet before Grampa got to me. My fist was clenched at my side. I could hear the sound of the dirt grinding between my teeth as I glared at that stinking horse.

Grampa tried to dust me off, only it hurt my shoulder when he brushed it. I yanked away from him.

"What'd I do?"

Grampa shrugged. "She's a trained cuttin' horse. You put your weight in one stirrup, she's gonna cut."

"All I did was look back at you."

Grampa nodded. "And when you looked back, you leaned in the right stirrup. And when you leaned in the right stirrup, she cut left. Just been trained. You didn't do anything wrong, and neither did she. Just been trained different. Neither one of you know what to expect from the other."

He took my hand, then walked over and picked up Beauty's reins.

"Figure that's enough riding for the first day." His

eyes seemed to twinkle. "Besides, I don't want you hurting my horse." He started off for the barn.

I rubbed my aching shoulder and felt my sore seat as I walked.

"Me hurt her?" I yelped. "I can't believe you said that, Grampa. She's thrown me off two times, and you're worried about me hurting her."

He only nodded. "Right. Fallin' off ain't good for a horse. Do it too often, and they get to figuring that's the way it's supposed to be. Then, first thing you know, they're doing things to get everybody to fall off. You done enough falling off for one day."

"Falling off, *falling off*? I wasn't falling off. I was thrown off!"

Grampa only shook his head and kept walking. "Wild horse will throw you off. Bucking stock will throw you off. Gentle, well-trained horse don't throw you. You either get off or, if you don't know what you're doing, you fall off. She's only doing what she's trained to do. Now come on. Let's get this saddle off her and—"

I didn't hear the rest of what Grampa was saying. I was so mad, I couldn't see straight. It wasn't right. I *did* know how to ride. It's just that Beauty was a wild, spooky, crazy horse who didn't even act like a horse. It was all her fault. Not mine.

I was mad!

Only I didn't even know what mad was. Not until I saw the way Mama acted after she came out to check on how we were doing.

CHAPTER 3

Grampa was just taking the saddle off Beauty when I heard Mama call from beside the barn, "You two still in there?"

I leaned around the edge of the fence post. "We're not *still* in here," I answered. "We're already finished."

Mama cocked an eyebrow as she went a couple of steps past where I was standing and climbed the wood fence. "Mighty short ride," she said. "Where's Beauty?"

Grampa had hung Beauty's reins over a nail just inside the barn while he went to put the saddle away. When Mama saw her, she walked right up to that old ugly horse and wrapped her arms around her thick, short neck. She started hugging her and petting her and telling her how clean and white and pretty she was.

Grampa came back, and we climbed to the top rail of the fence and sat. He popped his elbows on his knees and lit his pipe. All I could do was roll my eyes.

"This is almost sickening," I mumbled.

Grampa glanced over at me. "Huh?"

I shook my head. "Oh, nothing. Just talking to myself."

After Mama carried on over Beauty some more, she took the bridle off and came to where we were sitting on the fence.

I noticed that Mama's eyes were scrunched up and her lips were stretched together so tight they were turning white.

She walked right up to Grampa, put her hand on his knee, and in a real soft voice, like she was whispering so the old horse wouldn't hear, she said, "I'm going over to this Mr. Garrison's place and tell him *exactly* what I think of him. Did you see her? Her poor old ribs are sticking out! I bet he hasn't fed her for months."

I noticed how red her face was getting when she climbed over the corral fence.

"And anybody who'd starve a poor old horse like that ought to be whipped. I'd just like to get my hands on that dirty #&**#$#."

I felt my eyes pop wide open. As long as I could remember, I'd never heard my mama use words like the names she called that man. I didn't even think my mama knew words like she just used.

Grampa swung his legs around and jumped down from the top rail of the fence.

"Now hold on a second, Carol," he said. "Mike's been feeding her—"

Only Mama wasn't listening. She didn't even slow down. She marched off toward the road. Her feet were coming down so hard, the red Oklahoma dust puffed and belched up from under them in all directions.

Grampa took off after her.

I jumped down and took off after Grampa.

"I'm not even going to bother to talk to him," Mama snarled, up ahead of us. "Talk won't do any good with somebody as sorry as he must be. Just one good punch . . ."

Grampa started taking longer steps, trying to catch up to her. "Carol! You don't understand. Wait up. . . . Carol!"

I could see Mama shake her fist. "Just one punch —right in the mouth!"

Grampa started running. "Now, Carol."

I started running too. There was no way I was

going to get left behind. I couldn't believe it. Mama never talked about hitting anybody. Even when she and Daddy used to have their big fights, she just wasn't one for hitting. But here she was—my meek, mild, calm Mama—fixing to go beat up on some poor farmer because of a silly old horse.

Grampa had almost caught her when we rounded the corner of the barn, but then she stopped. A pickup was coming up the gravel driveway toward us. She hesitated just long enough for Grampa to catch her arm.

"Now Carol. You don't understand what you're talking about. Garrison's a good man. Beauty's an old horse. He's been feeding her and taking good care of—"

Right then Grampa saw the pickup coming, too. He stopped in the middle of his sentence. I caught up with them just in time to see his mouth flop open. His pipe fell out on the ground.

"Oh, my Lord," he gasped. "Not now!"

I picked Grampa's pipe out of the dust and handed it to him, only he didn't take it. He just stood there with his mouth gaping open, staring at the truck.

It was a big truck, one of those with the double cab and the four tires on the back underneath the big, wide fenders. It was bright red and shiny clean, except for the layer of dust that had settled on it from coming up our driveway. It stopped right next to where Mama and Grampa were scuffling with one another.

"Morning, Willie," a real deep but cheerful voice called to Grampa. "This must be your daughter and grandson you were telling me about."

I knew he was a big man, just seeing him as he sat there in his pickup. But when he climbed out and got himself all unfolded and standing up straight, I could hardly believe my eyes.

My daddy was six foot. To me, my daddy was a tall man. But this guy must have been a full head taller. He was big, too. His shoulders and chest were big enough for two men, not just one. He tapered down in kind of a V-shape to the longest legs I'd ever seen. He had on faded blue jeans and a huge pair of grungy, dusty, cruddy-looking cowboy boots that could have held both my feet, with enough room left over to wiggle my toes.

He moved with a long, smooth stride as he walked around the front of the truck to where I was standing with my mouth gaping open.

"You must be Luke," he said, smiling.

At least I thought he was smiling. I couldn't really tell for sure since his face was covered with a beard. It was a salt-and-pepper color, mostly black with a lot of white hairs mixed in and all swirling around. It was the same as his hair, at least what I could see of it. Most was hidden under the big crumpled straw cowboy hat he wore. His eyes were a blue gray, and they danced in his brown, rugged face.

I had to lean back to look up at him as he came closer.

"Willie, you told me your grandson was big and handsome. You weren't lying, not one bit."

I felt the heat running up my cheeks to my ears, turning my face red. Nobody, no stranger anyway, had ever called me handsome.

His huge hand almost swallowed mine as he took it and gave it a shake. His hands were rough and calloused, yet he didn't try to smash me like a lot of guys do when they shake hands. He was gentle and easy.

"It's a real pleasure to meet you, Luke."

Then he turned toward Mama and Grampa. "And you must be Carol."

Grampa jumped in front of him. He was so nervous, he reached up to take the pipe out of his mouth, not even remembering that I still had it.

"Er . . . ah . . . we're awful busy right now," Grampa stammered. "Ah . . . kind of a . . . family discussion. Why don't you come back later and ah . . . er . . ."

The big man motioned to his truck. "Had to bring

the old gal her feed. Only had two sacks left, so I went to the mill over in Verden real early this morning and had some ground up. I came to unload it for you. Figured while I was here, I'd meet your family. The way old Willie here's been bragging on you two is down right shameful."

I was standing behind him, but I could tell when he smiled, because his ears kind of raised his cowboy hat up.

"I thought you were just bragging," he went on. "Till now, that is. I can sure see where Luke got his good looks from. It's a real pleasure to meet you, ma'am."

He reached one of his huge hands right over Grampa's shoulder to shake hands with Mama. Mama didn't return his smile. Her face was red, but not on account of her being embarrassed by his compliments. She was red-faced on account of still being mad about her horse. And no matter how many nice things this guy had to say, she wasn't over her mad yet.

I couldn't help noticing the strange look on her face, almost like she was curious or suspicious about something.

"Aren't you going to introduce us, Daddy?"

I could see Grampa's mouth moving, but no words came out. He just stood there, trying to stay between them, with his mouth flopping and not a single sound coming to his lips.

The big man stretched his hand a little farther toward Mama.

"I'm Mike Garrison," he said. "Live on the ranch down the road there. I'm real pleased to meet you."

My eyes flashed wide open.

"Mike Garrison!"

I slapped a hand over my mouth to keep from yelling.

Mama almost smiled. It was a really weird, funny-looking smile. The breath caught in my throat. I couldn't move.

She scooted Grampa aside with her arm. Grampa's shoulders sagged. He looked helpless as he stepped out of the way, like he had done all he could and now it was too late.

Mama had her neck way back looking up at the big man. Ever so slowly, she looked down at the hand he was offering.

Then . . .

She doubled up her fist and slugged him, as hard as she could, right in the stomach.

I heard a little squeak. For a second I thought it was him. Then I realized the sound had come from me.

He didn't even flinch. Under his beard I could see

the confusion on his rugged face. I just knew he was going to reach out that big fist of his and squash my mama right into the red dust.

Instead, he looked at Mama with a puzzled frown. Then he looked at Grampa and back at Mama again. Finally, he glanced down at his own hand.

A silly grin came to his face, like maybe he was thinking Mama was really trying to shake hands and she'd just missed. He scooted his big paw over to where she'd popped him in the stomach and offered it to her again. At the same time he tipped his cowboy hat.

One of my hands was already over my mouth. When I saw what was going to happen, I slapped the other hand over my mouth too.

Mama slugged him in the stomach—again!

CHAPTER 4

Mama nestled into the corner of the couch. Her knees were tucked under her chin, and she was all scrunched up in a ball. Grampa paced back and forth across the living room in front of her.

"From the day you were born," he growled in his loudest voice, "from the very day you were born, I've been proud of you." He waved his arms in the air, making a big point of everything he said.

"I was proud of you when you took your first steps. I was proud of you when you rode your first horse. I was proud when you went to school for the very first time. I was proud when you got picked as head cheerleader. I was proud when you graduated. I was proud when you got married . . ." and under his breath he added, "even though I didn't much care for Jerry." Then, loud and yelling again, he continued: "I was proud of you when you got that job at the AT & T plant in Denver. I was proud of you when you gave me a grandson. I've always been proud of you. Always! *Always* . . . until *today*."

Mama tucked her chin farther down between her knees. She wouldn't look up at him.

"Never in my life—*never* have I been so ashamed of anyone. So ashamed and so embarrassed. Just think, my own daughter flies off the handle like that. Hits somebody! Shoot, you didn't even do stuff like that when you were in grade school. And the language . . . You sure didn't learn those names you called him from me. I ought to wash your mouth out with soap. No, I should have bent you over my knee and—"

"I'm sorry," Mama pleaded. "I just didn't understand." Her voice was soft and meek as a little kid's.

"No, you didn't understand," Grampa roared. "You wouldn't shut up long enough."

He started pacing again.

"Carol, that old horse of yours is twenty-seven years old. She's already lived four to six years longer than most horses ever do. You expect her to still look like a filly or something? I'm almost seventy. You didn't gripe and fuss about me not looking as young and spry as I did when I was forty. She's old! She looks old! She's lucky to be alive. How else could she look?"

His voice calmed a bit. He sat down on the far end of the couch from where Mama was.

"And that poor man. Why, Carol, he's nursed that old horse of yours like she was part of his family. Her stall's so clean you could eat off the floor. He keeps fresh straw in there. Must clean it out two, three times a day. He grinds her feed 'cause she's so old she can't digest regular feed and oats. He's taken her to the vet three times in the last two years to have her teeth ground so she can chew. He curries her and brushes her and keeps her almost as clean as her stall. And then . . . and then . . ."

His gravelly old voice started to rage again.

"Then you have the gall to punch him in the stomach and accuse him of starving her half to death and mistreating her and everything else you can think of to say to him."

"I didn't know, Daddy."

"No, you didn't know! You can't imagine how much what you said hurt that poor man."

Grampa just kept fussing and griping at Mama. Once, when she looked up, I could see a little tear running down her cheek.

Right then, I knew. . .

I didn't like Oklahoma. I didn't like Chickasha. I hadn't wanted to come here in the first place. Things were rough back in Denver. Times were hard, but Mama and I were together. We could have made it through the hard times, just the two of us.

Grampa wasn't being fair. Mama loved her old horse. He could have understood how *she* felt instead of fussing at her about how bad she'd made that Mike Garrison feel. He could have been fair.

Right then, I knew I was beginning to hate my grampa. He was mean and cruel and heartless, and he had no right saying mean things to my mama like that.

I wished she'd get up and tell him off. I wished she'd really let him have it, and then we'd pack our clothes and leave this hot, dry, stinking place and that mean, vicious tyrant who was my grandfather.

Two weeks later, I felt the same way.

Well, not quite the same. Maybe Grampa wasn't really mean and vicious. But I *did* wish we were away from him, back on our own again.

Lots had happened. Mama had gone over with Grampa to see Mr. Garrison and apologize for all the things she'd said. She'd ended up inviting him for supper one evening.

Even though he was big and rough and almost ugly, I kind of liked him. He laughed a lot and had a good sense of humor. Right about the time we were finishing up supper, he got to teasing Mama about what a good right hand she had.

She turned red. Everybody laughed, just a little. Then Mr. Garrison said something about never fighting with women, especially women as beautiful and attractive as she was.

I thought it was a really nice thing for him to say, only Mama got quiet and didn't talk much more through supper. After a while, she got up and started doing the dishes and just downright ignored him.

As Mr. Garrison was leaving, Grampa invited him back for supper the following week. But he said he couldn't. He was going out of town to look at some horses over in New Mexico and would be gone for the rest of that week and the following one. He said he'd take a rain check, whatever that meant. Then he thanked Mama for the supper and left.

It made me feel good that everything had been fixed up. Grampa wasn't fussing at Mama anymore, and she seemed happier now that she had apologized to Mr. Garrison. Things settled down really nice.

I got to ride Beauty during those two weeks, too. Every day after lunch, Grampa would put the saddle and bridle on her. The first week he wouldn't let me ride any place but in the pen and only with him watching.

I found that with Beauty I could do just about anything, as long as I did it slowly. If I pulled the reins easy, she wouldn't cut. If I leaned in one stirrup or the other, she would move sideways.

One day I dropped the curry comb, and without even thinking I reached down and got it. When I looked up, I was right square behind Beauty. Her hind feet were not more than a foot from my nose. Never once did she even act like she was going to kick me. I could have crawled underneath her stomach, and it wouldn't have bothered her.

By the end of that first week we were getting along really well. I could make her trot and even gallop without having to worry about being thrown off. I guess it took her that long to figure out we were just riding for the fun of it, not doing serious stuff like cutting cattle.

The beginning of the second week, Grampa decided I was big enough to saddle her myself. He helped me the first couple of times, and from then on he stood back and let me do it alone.

Along with saddling her, he let Beauty and me go outside the pen. But not without first giving me a long lecture about how old she was and how I needed to take it easy with her.

"She's old and her balance isn't as good as it used to be," he lectured. "Don't want you running her. Nothin' more than a slow trot. If you take her out to the south pasture, stick to the cow trails and the flat ground. Don't want you running up and down that canyon on the back part of the farm. And . . ."

Every time I got ready to ride, he'd go on and on until all I wanted to do was stick my fingers in my ears so I wouldn't have to listen to him anymore.

It got to where riding Beauty wasn't all that much fun. Fun was running and feeling the wind blow against my face, not easing along, worrying about how old my horse was. Now that we were used to each other, riding should be exciting, not cautious.

But she was old and slow.

We did have some fun, though. There was a big pond with tall shade trees. We would circle it and watch all the little green frogs go plop in the water when we came near. The black waterbugs would scurry away and go darting in every-which-direction when Beauty's big hoof flipped a dirt clod in the water.

We'd find cow trails to follow that wound around and across the pasture and through the blackjack trees and scrub oaks. We'd follow the trails into small clearings that were hidden, and sometimes we'd find a rabbit or some quail hiding along the way.

Even though Beauty and I had those good times, I started longing for a real horse that I could ride hard and fast, one that could gallop all day without working up a lather, a horse that could race across the fields with me and send the wind swirling through my hair.

During that two weeks Mama found a job. She worked as a part-time saleslady at a place called the Dixie. It was a clothing store in downtown Chickasha, right on Main Street. Mama was hired to help out on Fridays and Saturdays.

She said that the man who hired her told her that if she worked out all right, he'd hire her for two weeks while one of the other women took a vacation, and if that worked, he might find a place for her full-time.

Mama said it wasn't much, but it was a start. She was happy about it.

CHAPTER 5

"You've got to be the silliest-looking animal I've ever seen in my life."

Beauty ignored me. She didn't even look around. She was backed up to the big wooden post next to the gate. Her tail was cocked up and kind of over to one side. Her hind feet were beside her front ones, as she leaned her tail end way back to rub it on the gate post.

That was funny-looking enough, the way she was all scrunched up, scratching her hind end on the post. But what was funniest of all was her face.

Her eyes were kind of sleepy-looking and rolled back in her head. Her mouth was about half open. And her bottom lip kept flopping up and down like she was mumbling something to herself.

The goofy look on her face made me chuckle. I was enjoying just standing there watching her when all of a sudden:

B O O M !!!

I almost leapt out of my skin.

The loud boom scared Beauty, too. One second, she was bunched up, scratching her tail on the post. The next, she was about six feet away, after jumping and hitting the ground running.

Her tail was straight up in the air, and so were her ears. She ran a ways, stopped, and turned around. She looked at the barn and gave a loud snort. Then she lifted her tail and took off at a trot across the corral.

I could feel my legs shaking. I frowned, wondering what the loud noise was. Then:

B O O M !!!

This time I jumped.

I didn't land as far away from where I'd been as Beauty had. But when I came down, my legs were as tight as a drum and were ready to take me running back to the house.

Then, from inside the barn, I heard Grampa's voice muttering something. I couldn't tell what he was saying, but it was Grampa. At least, I thought it was.

"Grampa?"

More muttering.

"Grampa? Is that you?"

My legs were even more ready to take off for the house. There was a second of silence.

"Luke?" His voice was kind of far off, hard to hear. "Luke? You out there?"

"Grampa," I called toward the barn. "You all right? What happened?"

"Rats," he called.

I frowned.

"Rats?"

Grampa mumbled something else, but I couldn't make it out. I took a step toward the barn and opened the gate to the horse lot next to it. It went back under the barn so horses could come in out of the rain or the cold. Inside, there was a wood-rail fence. I climbed over it, stopping for a minute so my eyes could get used to the dark inside.

Except for the corner with the horse pen and a few feet around the edges, this whole end of the barn was stacked high with bales of hay. There was a wide pathway leading down the middle.

I could hear Grampa mumbling and making kind of a growling sound, so I walked along the pathway to where the noise was coming from. I walked clear to the other end of the barn before I found him. He was climbing down from a stack of hay bales, grunting and groaning with each step.

"You all right, Grampa?"

He glanced at me. "Just fine." He puffed. "Just getting old. Used to be I could scamper up and down these bales like a squirrel in a tree. Nowadays, it's a real struggle." He stopped a moment to catch his breath. "Here," he said. "Hold this."

I took the thing he handed me. It was a great big gun with two barrels. When Grampa let go of it, the thing was so heavy, it almost knocked me over.

"My ten-gauge," Grampa growled, taking the last step off the haystack.

I held my breath, just knowing he was going to fall flat on his back. But Grampa caught himself. He stood for a moment, panting.

"Used to be I could pick 'em off with a twenty-two. But that was back when I was younger, 'fore the eyes started going bad. Now I have to use the shotgun. Even so, I still miss 'em part of the time."

"Miss what?"

"Rats."

I felt my nose crinkle up. "Rats?"

He nodded. "Big rascals, too." With a jerk of his head, he motioned me to follow. "Come on, I'll show you."

I tagged along, wrestling and struggling with the big old shotgun with every step.

Grampa finally noticed all the trouble I was having.

"Here." He took the shotgun and showed me how to hold it. "You put one hand back here on the stock, by the trigger. The other goes way up here under the barrels. That way you can balance it. Got too much gun to just hold it by the butt like you were doing."

He gave back the shotgun. With my hands spread out like he showed me, it was a lot easier to carry. The thing was still awfully long and heavy, though.

I followed him over to a big wooden box at the side of the barn. He kicked the loose hay around for a moment with his foot.

"Ahh," he smiled. "Got ya!"

Grampa reached over and picked up an enormous, dead gray-brown rat. It looked just like a little house mouse, only it was about ten times as big. If I had seen it from far away, instead of up close, I'd probably have figured it was a cat or something. It was really that big.

Grampa held it upside down by its big old ratty tail. Just looking at it made my skin crawl.

He kicked around in the hay some more, like he was looking for something else. Then, with a sigh, he shook his head.

"Missed the other one. Gettin' blind as a bat. No

sense waitin' around. The other one won't be showin' itself, least for a couple of days. Let's go dump this one and put the gun up. Then we'll come back so you can ride Beauty."

The minute we got out of the barn, Grampa dropped the rat. He reached in his pocket and pulled out his old black pipe and lit it, then picked the rat up again.

"Never smoke in the barn," he told me. "Too much old dry hay and grain dust. Littlest old spark and that thing would go up like a torch."

I noticed how long Grampa's legs were and what big steps he took for an old man. By the time we got to the top of the hill behind the barn, I was panting for breath and might-near worn out.

"Ensilage pit," he said, tossing the dead rat in the long trench dug into the side of the hill. It was full of dead weeds and junk and paper and trash. It was deeper than I was tall and almost as long as the barn.

"Used to put ensilage in these things for feed over the winter. We'd cut corn or maize and grind the whole plant up as fodder for the cows."

I frowned. "What's fodder?"

"Feed," he went on. "Anyway, nobody's put up ensilage in these parts for a long time now. Ought to fill it in one of these days," he added, shrugging, "only it makes a right good trash dump."

He took the big shotgun from me.

"You know what?" he asked as I trailed along after him back toward the barn.

"What?"

"I ought to get my little twenty-two out and teach you how to use it. You could help keep those pesky rats out of the grain bin. Besides, old and feeble as I'm getting, I'm probably gonna break my neck one of these days trying to climb up and down those bales of hay."

"How come you do that?" I asked.

"Do what? Break my neck?"

"No. Climb up on the hay."

Grampa shrugged. "See better from up there. Then, too, you get down in the bottom of the barn, the rats can see you. Don't come out and move around."

I glanced at the big double-barreled shotgun in Grampa's hand. It was old and rusty-looking. There were two big hammers to pull back with your thumb.

"How come you don't just poison them or set traps or something like that?"

Grampa stopped square in his tracks. His wrinkled face was stern. But then it softened to an easy smile.

"Well, I'll tell you," he said, starting on toward the barn once more. "When your grandmother and I first moved here, she had this calico cat."

He gave a little chuckle. I saw a big puff of blue-white smoke roll out of his pipe and up his forehead.

"Still think she thought more of that cat than she did of me. Anyway, I set some poison out for the rats. Still don't think the cat got into it. I reckon she got her a mouse or somethin' that'd eaten the stuff. Anyhow, she died. Your grandmother was heartbroken. Never did use poison after that. Your grandmother always had some stray cat she took a liking to. Figured if I set a trap, it'd be my luck to end up with a cat she favored instead of catchin' a rat like I wanted. So . . ." He patted the big shotgun. "I decided shooting them was the best way."

Grampa stopped again. He turned toward me. "Here."

I took the big, heavy shotgun.

Grampa smiled. "You handle that right good. Tell you what. Why don't we go back to the dump and load 'er up. Got a powerful kick, but I figure you're man enough to handle it. You want to learn how to shoot?"

I thought about how heavy it was and how much it must kick and how loud the boom had been that I'd heard earlier.

It took about a half-second before I answered, "No. I'd rather ride Beauty."

For a minute, I was afraid I might have hurt

Grampa's feelings. He seemed awfully proud of that old shotgun and awfully interested in showing me how to use it.

But Grampa only chuckled. He took the shotgun from me and led the way back to the barn.

CHAPTER 6

I was smiling and happy and feeling good inside, just thinking about how Grampa had said that I was "man enough" to handle that big shotgun. But by the time we reached the barn, it took Grampa only a second to knock the good feeling clear out of me.

"Luke, look at this!"

His soft, cheerful voice had changed to a roar. Like a mad lion in a circus cage, he was growling and snapping.

"Left this gate wide open! Look at it! Don't you ever *ever* leave this gate open again. Do you understand?"

All his yelling and loud racket made me take a step back. My shoulders tightened as I stood real straight.

"I didn't mean to, Grampa. When I heard the shotgun . . . and I didn't know what it was . . . Then you shot again . . . and . . . and . . . well, it scared me and I forgot."

His eyes tightened down to tiny slits in his wrinkled old face.

"Don't you *ever* forget again," he growled like he was fixing to eat me up. "You always close this gate, no matter what!"

I bristled. "I don't know why you're making such a big fuss, Grampa. I didn't mean to leave it open. I just forgot. It's no big deal . . . I . . ."

"No big deal??? No big *deal!*"

He was practically screaming at me. "You know what would happen if that horse got out and wandered down to the cattle guard? You ever seen a horse with a leg caught in a cattle guard? I have! When you come through this gate . . ."

I turned and started walking away.

"Where you think you're going?" he snapped.

I didn't look back.

"I'm going to the house." I wanted to stick my tongue out, but I didn't. "I don't want to ride that stinking old horse anyway."

I'll show him, I thought. I don't have to stand around and get yelled at. I'll just show him.

I would have, too, only right about then, he

latched onto one of my ears. He grabbed hold so hard, he almost yanked me clean off my feet. He spun me around, by the ear, and stuck my nose against the gate.

"Lock it!"

I tried to pull away, but Grampa just squeezed harder on my ear.

"Lock the gate!"

I slipped the thumb bolt in place. He tugged just a little, turning my head toward the road.

"Come on."

He let go. I started to run for the house, then decided it wouldn't do any good. He'd only come after me. So instead of running off, I followed him down the dusty road.

I didn't like it, though. Not one little bit.

It was about a quarter-mile from the barn to the gravel section line. Some twenty feet from the road, Grampa stopped and motioned me to come look at this big metal contraption in our drive.

"Cattle guard," he announced.

There were about eight metal pipes running across the road, with spaces in between them. The spaces were big enough for my whole foot, shoe and all, to slide into. I stepped a little closer and looked down.

There was kind of a trench running under the thing. The bright Oklahoma sun was straight up over the top of my head, so I could see clean to the bottom.

I decided against walking out on it for a closer look. If I slipped off one of the bars and fell in between, I'd go clear to the bottom.

"Cattle guard is built to keep cows in and still have a place that you can drive over without having to stop and get out to open a gate," Grampa explained, his voice calm now.

"Most usually, cows won't try to cross the thing 'cause the spaces in between the bars spook them. Cows know they're likely to slip and get a hoof caught. Sometimes, though, a young calf or a spooked heifer will try to jump the thing. It always ends up stuck in it.

"Thing with a cow, their bones are tough and limber. Ninety-nine times out of a hundred, they work themselves out with nothing worse than a bad scare, which keeps them from trying it again. Horse is different! Bones are longer. More brittle. Horse ever gets in this cattle guard, it . . . well, it breaks its legs all to pieces. Nothing . . . nothing you can do for it. Nothing but . . ."

His voice trailed off. I couldn't help noticing a sad, faraway look in his eyes. His voice got softer, and he wiped his mouth when he took his old black pipe out. Something was hurting him.

"I'm sorry I left the gate open." That's all I could think of to say.

Grampa looked down at me with those big, deep, brown eyes. He almost smiled, but it was a sad smile.

"I'm sorry, too," he whispered. "I shouldn't have yelled at you. It's just . . . I'm sorry."

There was kind of a lump in my throat, but I swallowed it down. I still don't know why I said what I did. Maybe it was the look in Grampa's eyes. Maybe it was the way he stared at the cattle guard, like it was something far, far away, instead of right here beside us. Maybe it was the way he wiped his face again with the cuff of his old flannel shirt.

"Was it your horse, Grampa?"

He gave a little sigh, then walked over to a big cottonwood tree close by the road. He leaned his shotgun against the tree before sitting down in the shade.

I walked over and sat beside him. "Was it, Grampa?"

He cleared his throat, a sound like gravel rattling in a pan.

"Yeah," he answered. "His name was Ribbon. My parents got him for me when I was eleven. Tennessee Walker. Proud and straight and tall, like riding on the wind."

His voice was tight, but a little smile curled his lips

as he talked about his horse. "I did a lot of growing up on that old horse's back. More like a friend than a horse. I mean . . . well, I used to talk to him, tell him secrets about the way I felt and what I wanted to be when I grew up. All that sort of stuff.

"Anyhow, when I went off to college, I kinda forgot about him. Didn't think about him much till after your grandmother and I were married and we had your mama and moved back here to live on the farm.

"Ribbon was about as old as Beauty, then. He was getting sway-backed and slowing down. But your mama took a liking to him, and since he was old and gentle, she sort of took him over as her own. I don't know whether it was me who left the gate open after coming back from shooting rats, or if it was your mother who forgot to shut it after she got through riding. Anyway, don't make no difference . . ."

His voice trailed off. The tobacco had gone out in his pipe. Grampa tamped his finger down into the bowl and lit the thing again.

"Big storm come up that night. Wind and lightning and hail. Old Ribbon must have got spooked. Gate was open and he took off running. Horses do that when they're scared. Just natural for them.

"Oil company had just put the cattle guard in so they could start drilling that well on the back of our place. You've seen it, I'm sure."

I nodded, remembering the big black pump I'd found one time when Beauty and I were out exploring.

"Anyhow, Ribbon either didn't know the cattle guard was there, or couldn't see it . . ."

His voice got really tight again. It was a long time before he started talking once more.

"I heard him screaming. It's a sound I'll never forget as long as I live. Never knew a horse could scream. Like a woman screaming, only higher, louder. And you can feel the hurt in it. Feel it almost as strong as if the hurting was in you. Had both legs in there. Both broken and bleeding and him struggling to get loose and . . . and screaming all the time. Screaming and hurting and . . . I never knew how much I loved that old horse. How close I was to him, how much he meant to me. I never knew till I had to stick that shotgun to his head and pull the trigger . . . and kill my old horse."

I heard my grampa sniff. We sat there for a while. I didn't look at him. He didn't look at me.

After a minute or two he made a grunting sound and got up. He turned to me and smiled. "Like I said, I'm sorry I yelled at you about leaving the gate open. I should have explained why I was mad back at the barn. I always get busy and don't take time to explain things. Guess I ought to."

I smiled back.

"It's okay, Grampa. I understand now. I won't *ever* leave that gate open—promise!"

I made an *X* over my heart with my finger.

CHAPTER 7

"I don't understand, Grampa."

He cleared his throat. "So what's there to understand? I went over to Mike's place this morning and brought her back. Her name's Lady. She's Beauty's filly. She's eight years old, and her father was a champion cutting horse. I got the bridle and the saddle on her. All you got to do is climb up and ride."

I put my fists on my hips and glared at his mean-looking, wrinkled face.

"But I don't want to ride *her,* Grampa. I want to ride Beauty. I like Beauty. I even know how to saddle her by myself now. You showed me how about a month ago, remember? I want to ride Beauty!"

He stuck a match to his old black pipe. The blue-white smoke rolled back over his forehead in a big cloud.

"We ain't gonna argue about it, Luke," he growled in his deep, gravely voice. "It's time you learned how to ride a real horse. A young horse you can gallop and run and don't have to be so careful with."

I clenched my fists at my sides. I felt my bottom jaw set as I glared at my grampa.

He glared back at me.

"Well?"

I looked up at the horse beside us. Lady wasn't at all like Beauty. The first thing I noticed were her eyes. They had a wide, almost glazed look to them. Kind of "crazy eyes." Beauty's eyes were soft and gentle, like she was. This horse, Lady, seemed nervous and tense. She kept shuffling her feet and looking around, moving all the time. Lady was a dark copper color and full of muscles and big. Beauty was white and narrow and soft.

I stood there, watching her wiggle and jerk. I remembered how bad I wanted a "real" horse. I remembered how I thought about it, especially when Beauty and I were exploring the cow trails for the first time and when Grampa was lecturing me about how I had to be careful with her. During those speeches, a real horse is what I wanted more than anything in the world.

But now. . .

I don't like the looks of her, I thought. She's not nice like Beauty. She scares me.

I frowned. Being scared or chicken is something guys always worry about. When you're a boy, you're supposed to be brave and courageous. Only I sure didn't want to be on that horse.

"Well?" Grampa repeated.

I squinted my eyes and scowled at him. Grampa only smiled.

There was no arguing with him. He was as stubborn and grumpy and mean as anybody who ever walked the face of this earth.

All right, I told myself. If that's what he wants, I'll show him. I'm not scared. I'm as brave as anybody. I'll show him I can ride that stinking horse. And if she throws me off—well, that'll show him I was right all along and he should have left me alone and let me ride Beauty, like I wanted to.

I felt real cocky when I held Lady's reins on the saddle horn and put my foot in the stirrup. I bounced a couple of times before I could get up enough to throw my leg over her back and plop down in the saddle.

Either way, I was going to show him.

But when I got on Lady's back, I didn't want it to be "either way." I wanted to ride her. I wanted to show Grampa I could.

Being on Lady was a lot different from being on Beauty. Beauty was skinny, and my legs hung down by her sides. Lady was big and hard and round and my legs kind of stuck out on either side of her. Beauty was relaxed and slow and easy. Lady was jittery. Instead of standing with her head down and looking at me with sleepy eyes, she was alert. Her feet moved real quick, and she was so full of energy, it seemed like she might explode any second.

I would take it slow and easy at first. I'd be extra careful.

Don't kick her, I told myself. Don't jerk the reins. Just take everything nice and easy and slow.

But I was so scared and worked up and nervous and mad at Grampa, I guess I was hanging on tighter with my knees than I intended to.

Lady took off!

I had to pull the reins really hard to stop her. She stopped so quickly, I almost fell over on her neck. Then, when I let go, I was still squeezing too hard with my legs, and she took off again.

I jumped off.

I decided it was better to land on my feet than on my head or my bottom. Lady went a couple of steps, then looked back at me.

I turned to sneer at Grampa. I showed him, I thought. I showed him that she's too crazy for me to ride. Now, he'll have to let me ride Beauty.

The red dust puffed under Grampa's feet as he stormed toward us. The smoke was pouring out of his black pipe so hard, he reminded me of an old steam engine rolling down a track.

"That's it. Get on her! We're going to Mike."

My mouth flopped open. I shook my head.

"I . . . I can't ride her. I'll ride Beauty. I . . ."

Grampa didn't listen. He grabbed me under the arms and threw me on her back.

I started to swing my leg over and get off. "I don't want to ride her, Grampa. Really . . . I—"

"You stay on that horse or I'll tie you on," he threatened. "We're gonna take both of you over to Mike and see what he can do with you."

I started crying. I don't really know why. I didn't get hurt, but I was mad—mad because I couldn't ride her and mad because Grampa was making me and mad because I was scared of her and mad at myself because I couldn't stay on her and mad at her because she wouldn't let me—everything was all mixed up inside.

Maybe I *was* a coward. Maybe I was just mad. Maybe . . .

Grampa led Lady down the road. There was a gate next to the cattle guard. He opened it and then closed it behind us.

I just hoped nobody came along. I didn't think I could stand it if somebody drove by and saw Grampa leading me on that horse like I was some little kid who couldn't ride by myself.

That'd be so embarrassing, I'd just die!

CHAPTER 8

From our house, I'd seen Mike Garrison's big barn almost a half mile away. I figured it was full of hay for feeding his stock, just like ours. But when we got to the barn and Grampa led me through the big open doors, I found out it wasn't for hay at all.

It was an indoor arena that was empty except for the plowed, dirt floor. A wooden fence went around the inside edge, leaving a huge circle in the middle. At the corners and behind the fence were wooden seats, kind of like bleachers around a basketball court, but these were only in the corners.

There were two horses tied to the fence on the side where we were. Out in the middle, I could hear a noise, but it was so dark I couldn't see well. I blinked a couple of times.

Just about the time my eyes adjusted to the dark, I saw this horse bouncing up and down. Then this big man went sailing through the air and landed flat on his face in the plowed dirt.

I got off Lady.

"I think I like riding in Colorado better," I said. "Up there we spend most of the time *on* the horse. Seems like with Oklahoma-type riding, you spend most of your time on the ground."

Grampa tried to keep a straight face, only he started giggling. Then before he could help it, his giggles turned into a deep, roaring laugh that seemed to rattle the huge tin barn that surrounded the riding arena.

The big man who was lying facedown in the dirt got up. Dusting himself off, he came over to us.

As he got closer, Grampa tried to straighten up and quit laughing. But the harder he tried to quit, the more tickled he got. And the more tickled he got, the harder he laughed, until I was afraid he was going to bust plumb open.

I took a step back when Mike Garrison stopped right in front of Grampa. Even covered with dust, there was a hard look on his face. His nose was crooked, like it had been broken at least once or twice, and there were little scars running above both eyebrows. Still, there was a softness to his blue-gray eyes—a tender gentleness that I could almost feel.

When he spoke, his deep, smooth voice sounded like distant thunder rolling through a night sky.

"Fine neighbor you turned out to be, Willie Evans. Go to visit you and you sic your daughter on me. Then, you come for a visit here and laugh yourself silly 'cause I get thrown off a horse. You always treat neighbors like that?"

Grampa stopped laughing. He looked up at the big man.

"No, Mike, I don't," he answered in a stern tone. Then, he made a snorting sound and started chuckling again. "Not ordinarily—except when somebody looks as silly as you just did."

He turned away and put his hand over his mouth, only you could still see and hear his laughing.

The big man's mouth tugged up until his smile was almost stretching his beard clean up to his ears. Still, he tried to look mean and sound tough.

"You didn't hear me laughing at you the day you got your pant leg hung in the spring-tooth."

Grampa gave a little snort.

"Yeah. But that's only 'cause you thought I'd cut my leg off, and it scared you."

Mike nodded.

"Might-near did, too."

Grampa only shrugged. Then he told Mike about me falling off Lady and how he figured I was getting scared of her (which was right). And he explained what I'd said when we came in the door and Mike was flying through the air.

They both had another good laugh. Mike said that he was starting a "beginner's class" next Monday. He told Grampa that between now and then he'd try to ride Lady some more and gentle her down.

"Think I'll start Luke on one of my other horses," he said. "Even after I gentle Lady, she's still trained for cutting. Need to work some of it out of her."

"Need to work on both the horse and the kid," Grampa added. "Think these beginner lessons for Luke will help? Think you can turn him into a good rider?"

"I *am* a good rider," I mumbled under my breath.

Neither one of them heard me.

"What grade you gonna be in next year, Luke?" Mike asked.

"I'll be in sixth grade. Why?"

He smiled.

"There are about six people in the class who have signed up. Memory serves me, I think there's a girl named Beth and a boy by the name of Joshua who are gonna be sixth-graders next year. Might even be in some of your classes when school starts. Be nice to make a couple of school friends during the summer."

I nodded. Maybe this riding class wouldn't be so bad after all. Making new friends would be fun. Besides, it would be a lot nicer having Mike Garrison teach me how to ride than Grampa.

The way Grampa had treated me today made those old feelings about Mama and me being on our own again come flooding back. It made me wish she would hurry up and find a *good* job, so we could get away from Grampa and not have to put up with him anymore.

CHAPTER 9

I'd never seen a day so still since I'd come here. The surface of the pond was like a mirror. There wasn't a ripple on it.

The willow trees whose long, limber branches bobbed and swept at the edges of the water stood perfectly still. The limbs didn't even quiver.

As Beauty and I circled the pond a few times, I couldn't help noticing how hot and sticky I felt. The Oklahoma wind was always blowing, always kicking up the dust. Without it to cool things off, it was downright miserable. The water didn't look miserable though. It looked clear and blue and *cool*.

I stopped Beauty under the shade of a big cottonwood.

"Mama and Grampa would kill me if they ever found out," I told Beauty, shaking my head.

Beauty tugged at the reins, trying to reach the green grass at her feet. I loosened my grip and let her bend over to graze.

"Then again, if they didn't find out . . ."

I got off Beauty. I tied the reins loosely around the saddle horn so she could still reach down to eat grass.

"You're not gonna tell, are you?"

She chomped up another mouthful of grass.

"Okay. Good. You won't tell. I won't tell. Then they'll never find out."

A small creek fed the pond. I took my clothes off and waded out. The bottom was sandy. I couldn't believe how clear the water was. I could hold my hands down at my sides and still see the dirt under my fingernails.

It was kind of a strange little pool, a place where the water was blue and clear, instead of red and muddy like other ponds on Grampa's farm. I splashed and swam and laughed. Beauty acted like she didn't care if the water was nice or not. She just kept chomping the tall grass in the meadow beneath the huge trees.

I splashed some more. The water was cool. I felt fresh and clean all over. I felt free as a fish in that little pool.

* * *

Grampa opened the door to my room. He pitched my shirt so it landed beside me on the bed.

I gulped. He stood there a moment, then crooked his finger at me to come to him. Holding the shirt, I walked over to where he stood.

"Yours?"

I nodded, looking down at the floor.

"You got it all wadded up in a ball. Open it up."

Slowly, I did like my grampa said. There was a big, muddy hoofprint right square in the middle where that dumb old Beauty had stepped while I was swimming.

"You see that?" Grampa asked.

Again, I nodded.

"Got one on your chest to match it?"

I shook my head.

"Then it must have been off when it got stepped on, right?"

I nodded.

"Pond?"

I quit staring down at my scruffy old tennis shoes. I looked Grampa square in the eye. Only the mean, angry look I expected to see wasn't there. Instead his eyes almost seemed to sparkle, and he was trying hard to keep from busting out in a big smile.

With a quick jerk of his head, he motioned me to

follow. At the door to my room he looked both ways, like he was checking to make sure Mama wasn't around. We trotted down the hall to the laundry room. Once there, he closed the door behind us and took a bottle from one of the shelves.

"Prewash," he said, squirting some of the stuff on my shirt. Then he tossed it to me. "Here. Rub it together till the hoofprint is mostly gone."

I started scrubbing while Grampa dug in the wash basket.

"You gonna hide something, you got to know the system. First off, your mom usually leaves stuff in the washer till she's got enough for a load. Blue jeans and bright red stuff, she does separately. Everything else goes in together. That shirt's white."

He picked up a handful of clothes and pitched them in the washer.

"Don't put it on the bottom. If for some reason she takes stuff out, she'll spot it when she picks it up. Here."

He reached out, and I handed him the shirt. He rubbed the shirt together a few more times, then held it out to look at it.

"Not bad. Best we can do, I guess."

He stuffed it in the washer and put another two more handfuls of clothes on top of it.

"Leave the lid up. She only closes it when the thing's on."

He opened the door and looked both ways again, then jerked his head for me to follow. He went back down the hall to the bathroom. Once there, he closed the door behind us and locked it. After digging around under the cabinet for a while, he came up with a blue squirt bottle. Then, he found a bottle of hydrogen peroxide and a bottle of alcohol. He put the peroxide in the squirt bottle.

"Your mother finds out about you swimming in that pool, she'll beat your butt till it's as blue as your jeans. She finds out I been helping you, I won't be much better off. Still . . ." he stroked his chin a couple of times. "Never known a boy yet who could pass up skinny-dippin' in that pool on a hot summer day."

He motioned me to come stand by the sink. When I got there, he grabbed the top of my head and tilted it to the side.

"Water's clear," he said. "But there's lots of microscopic critters in it. Whenever you get back, put a squirt of hydrogen peroxide in your ears."

I felt the cold liquid dripping in my ear. He turned my head the other direction and squirted the other ear full. The rest that was in the bottle, he squirted out into the sink. Next, he stuck the alcohol in the squirt bottle.

"Always use the hydrogen peroxide, then the alcohol. There's some kind of fungus infection that can get in your ears. Your Uncle David came down with it once. It almost drove the doctor crazy till we finally found out he was swimming in that pool. Anyway, this will keep you from getting it. Got any cuts or scratches, wouldn't hurt to squirt them, too."

He flipped my head way over and filled one ear. The alcohol ran out of my ear and down my cheek, right into my mouth. It was the most gosh-awful stuff I ever tasted.

I gagged and tried to spit it out.

"You'll get where you can squirt and tilt your head so that won't happen," Grampa said. "For now, hush! Your mom's taking a nap. You get to coughing and sputtering, you'll wake her up, for sure."

He tilted my head over and squirted the other ear. Even with my mouth clamped shut, the taste of the alcohol snuck into one corner. I spit and wiped my face.

"Pond's clear and nice," Grampa said, putting the bottles away. "Been here for nearly sixty years and never seen a poisonous snake around this place. Still, don't hurt to keep your eyes open."

He thumped the cabinet with his finger.

"Squirt bottle's in here. You know where the peroxide and the alcohol are."

I nodded.

"All right. Don't forget to use them. Another thing. You got less chance of getting your clothes stepped on if you hang 'em in a tree. Shake 'em out good. Lots of wasps and spiders around that pond. And *be careful!*"

I smiled at him.

"I will."

He unlocked the door and looked both ways.

"Come on," he whispered with that twinkle in his eye. "It's almost time to get over to Mike's for your riding lesson."

I patted Grampa's shoulder. "Thank you, Grampa."

He swatted me playfully on the bottom. "Scat."

CHAPTER 10

Mama was on the phone when I got to the living room. She had a big smile on her face and was nodding at the receiver.

"I'll be happy to," she said. "Starting Wednesday? Eight-thirty?" She nodded again, said thank you, and hung up.

"That was Mr. Miller at the Dixie," she told me. Her voice was real excited and bouncy. "He wants me to work full time for the next four weeks while some of the other women are on vacation. And like he mentioned before, he said if I work out okay, it'll be a permanent job."

Grampa came through about then. Mama told him, too. Then she asked us if we wanted pizza for lunch.

"Not today," Grampa growled. "I need to get out in the pasture and work on that blasted hay baler. Dumb thing's broken down again. Just put mine in the fridge, and I'll eat it when I get back."

He went off muttering to himself about the hay baler. Mama got the pizza from the freezer. I got a little package of pepperoni out of the fridge and spread the pieces on before she put the pizza in the oven.

"I never put enough pepperoni on these things," Mama said. "You do a very artistic job."

We watched TV until the buzzer went off. When we finished eating, Mama reminded me of my one o'clock riding class at Mike's. I put on the new boots that Grampa and Mama had bought for me in town. They didn't hurt my feet at all. Leastways, not until I left the house and started walking toward Mike's place.

"You be careful around those horses," Mama called after me.

"I will."

Beauty had rolled while I was in the house. Her clean, white coat was all covered with dust. She had kind of a muddy spot where the saddle had been. When I walked past her corral, she came over, like she was expecting me to feed her some of the ground oats and stuff Mike had brought.

I did.

"You're the best horse I ever knew," I told her as I set the bucket down. "Even if you do step on my clothes. You're okay and so is Grampa."

Even after stopping to feed Beauty, I still got to Mike's place about the time all the other people did. We sat on some wood bleachers in the corner of the big, open arena. Mike had eight horses tied to the wood rail.

One of them was Lady. I just knew he was going to make me ride her. I just knew she'd throw me off, and I'd make a fool of myself in front of all these people. I held my breath when Mike walked up to her.

"This is Lady," he told the class. "I'm going to be working with her and demonstrating the things I want you to do with your horses."

A sigh of relief whooshed out of my chest.

"All the other horses are very gentle and well trained," Mike went on. "I want you to come pick out one to work with."

Nobody moved.

"Come on." Mike waved his huge hand. "Find one you like the looks of, and I'll show you what to do next."

Finally, everybody got up and started over to the

horses. There were two women, about Mama's age. They got the horses on either side of Lady. A mother with her little boy stood beside two paint horses. I walked over next and stood in front of a big black horse. A boy with really thick glasses got the brown horse closest to me. And a girl with long blond hair and blue eyes got the spotted horse on the end.

"Can everybody hear me all right?" Mike called.

We all turned to look at him and nodded.

"Good. Let's get started."

He showed us how to put the halter on our horses and how to tie the rope around a post so the horse couldn't get it loose, but we could, real quick, if we needed to. It was a loop sort of thing, and all you had to do was pull one end and it came right off. We needed practice with that, so Mike came by and helped each one of us.

While I was waiting for my turn, the guy next to me walked over to where I was.

"Hi." He smiled. "My name's Joshua. What's yours?"

"Luke."

"What grade are you in?"

"I'll be in sixth when school starts."

He frowned. "How come I never saw you last year?"

"We just moved here from Denver."

He looked me up and down, then smiled again. "You play football?"

I shrugged. "Yeah. We didn't have real teams or anything, but there was a vacant lot back home where we used to play after school."

He reached out and took hold of my wrist. Then he turned my hand over.

"You got big hands. I bet you're a wide receiver, right?"

I looked down at my hand.

"Well, I used to run out for passes and stuff, if that's what you mean."

He slapped me on the shoulder.

"I knew it," he said. "You're a wide receiver. We got a Mighty-Mite football league in Chickasha. Our coach has been looking for a good pass receiver. I bet—"

He stopped talking because Mike came up to help him with the knot. After that, Mike showed us how to curry and brush. Then we practiced putting the bridle on.

In between times, Joshua came over to visit, or I went over to where he was. I found out that he was the quarterback for his team. He knew just about everything there was to know about football. Besides that, he was fun to talk to. It didn't take long for us both to start really liking each other.

Mike told us that we were not supposed to walk in front of our horses. He said that if a horse gets spooked, its natural instinct is to lunge forward. If you're walking under its neck, you can either get squashed against the corral or get run over. He showed us how to walk up close behind a horse. That way, if the horse kicked, you wouldn't get hurt. He said that if you're close, you just get shoved, but if you're back a little and it kicks, you can really get busted.

When we were all finished, everybody followed Mike to go and put their horses up.

The corrals were in a smaller barn behind the big arena. There was a hallway down the center with stalls on either side. When Mike put Lady in her pen, I couldn't help noticing this little white horse down at the end.

It started whinnying and bucking and jumping up and down. It would race out the door to a small exercise pen, then come tearing back in and whinny some more. After I put my horse in his stall, I went to stand by Mike and watch the little white horse.

"Is that a wild horse?" I asked.

Mike smiled. "No. Just young. I only started breaking her last week."

"Why is she acting like that?"

Mike pointed his thumb at Lady. "Just saying 'Hi' to her mother, I guess."

"That's Lady's colt?"

"It's a filly," Mike corrected. "A boy horse is called a colt. A girl horse is a filly. And yes, that's Lady's filly."

I tilted my head to the side. "How come she's white? Lady is kind of a copper color and real dark."

Mike put an arm on my shoulder and started back to the arena where the others had gone. "Takes after her grandmother I guess. Come on. I need to tell the class what we're going to do tomorrow."

As soon as I got home, I fed Beauty and told her about everything that had happened at Mike's. I told her what I learned. I told her about Joshua. I even told her about the girl with blond hair and blue eyes. Joshua told me that her name was Beth. I thought she was cute, only I would never tell anybody that except Beauty.

The next day I told her about putting the saddles on and about the mother and her son. The boy was younger than me, and he went around acting dumb and scared all the time. But I don't think he really was. He just wanted his mom to do things for him. I also told her about the two women and how they kept trying to get Mike to come over and show them stuff.

They kept asking him really dumb questions, and they giggled a lot. I think they were flirting with him, because once when they called, he kind of rolled his eyes at me.

I went over to get Beauty's feed. One of the sacks was almost empty, so I picked it up. When I did, something caught my eye.

A rat!

A huge, gigantic rat was hiding under the sack. He glared up at me with his beady, ratty eyes. His scaly, ratty tail was curled up behind him. Then he ran.

I yelled and jumped. Beauty's feed went flying all over the barn.

CHAPTER 11

"Pull the butt in close against your shoulder. Lay your cheek down tight along the stock so you can look at those two sights I showed you."

I held the big, heavy shotgun out at arm's length.

"But Grampa, you said it kicked."

He took the pipe out of his mouth. "It does. But it kicks less if you hold it tight than it does if you don't."

I did like Grampa said.

"Now put the middle of the can right in line with the sights."

I closed my left eye and squinted with my right till the two little sight beads on top of the shotgun were lined up and the one on the tip of the barrel was square in the middle of the can.

"Okay," I mumbled out of the corner of my mouth. The other side of my mouth was pushed up against the stock of the shotgun so hard I couldn't talk out of it.

Grampa made that sound of gravel rattling in a pan when he cleared his throat.

"Now, remember to squeeze the trigger. Don't yank it."

I started to squeeze. When I did, I leaned my head away from the shotgun. I knew it was going to kick me, so I guess I pulled it a little ways from my shoulder, too.

I yanked the trigger. Nothing happened. I yanked again. Still nothing.

I held the gun away from me and looked at it.

"Forgot to cock it," Grampa growled.

The two big hammers he had told me about were still sitting flat against the back of the gun. I turned toward Grampa.

"These things?"

"Don't you do that," he almost screamed. "Turn that back around."

I noticed that when I turned, the barrel of the gun went toward him.

"I'm sorry," I said. "But it's not cocked."

Grampa was sitting on the edge of the ensilage pit with his legs dangling over the side. He started to get up, but he didn't.

"Don't matter. Gun that ain't loaded or one that ain't cocked are the ones that usually kill people. You *never* point a gun at anyone."

I frowned.

"What do you mean one that ain't loaded kills people? How can . . ."

"People are careful with a loaded gun. But one they think is unloaded or on safety sometimes makes them careless. You get careless, somebody gets hurt.

"Guns are made for killing. That's the only thing they're for. And they don't give a flying-flip what they kill. It's the people handling them who have to take all the responsibility. You *always* handle a gun like your life and the life of anybody around you depends on how safe and careful you are, 'cause it does."

I nodded my head.

"I understand, Grampa. I'll be careful."

He smiled. "Okay. Try it again."

I had to use both thumbs to pull the hammer back. I pulled it all the way, just like Grampa had showed me. I squeezed it tight against my shoulder. I put my cheek down against the side of it, only when I started to squeeze, I guess I scooted it out a ways from my shoulder. What happened next went so fast, I can't rightly remember how and what came first.

There was a loud "BOOM". Then something slammed against my shoulder and bounced against my cheek. I felt myself falling backward, and the next thing I knew, I was lying on the ground with my feet up over my head, like I was about to do the bicycle exercise in gym class.

I rolled on my side, then crawled to my knees, looking around to see what had happened. Grampa's shotgun was right there beside me. The can, down in the ensilage pit, was just where I left it—not a mark on the thing.

My shoulder hurt something terrible. I rubbed it. The whole world was sort of spinning. I shook my head.

I heard a snorting sound, so I looked around to see where the noise was coming from. Grampa clamped a hand over his mouth, but his sides were bouncing up and down.

I got to my feet. I put my fists on my hips. He was working so hard at holding his laughter in that his eyes bugged out.

I glared at him. He put his other hand over his stomach, like it was hurting.

I cocked my head to the side.

"What's so funny?"

That did it!

Grampa burst out laughing. He flopped backward onto the ground and started rolling from side to side.

The way Grampa was acting was really disgusting. I let him know how I felt by the look on my face, but that just made him laugh more.

I was making all the right faces and acting mad, only I really wasn't. Inside, I was laughing along with him.

Grampa sat up. He pinched his nose with his finger and thumb.

"I knew you were man enough to handle it," he snorted. "First time I shot the thing, I rolled clean over, twice. You only rolled once."

Grampa finally got to his feet. He dusted himself off and hunted around to find where his pipe had fallen while he was laughing. Then he came over and picked up the shotgun.

"You mean that's the way you're supposed to shoot a shotgun the first time?" I asked.

Grampa shook his head.

"No, it's not supposed to knock you rolling. But I don't know of any kid who doesn't move the gun away from his shoulder the first time he shoots the thing. You know it's gonna kick, so you try to scoot it away. Only, when you do that, instead of rocking you a little, it kicks the snot out of you. I guess it's the only way to learn to hold it tight."

He walked around behind me. He put the gun against my shoulder and showed me again how to hold it.

"Lean into it a little. Be sure it's pulled tight."

I pulled the thing against my shoulder as hard as I could.

This time, when I squeezed the trigger, the gun rocked me. It kind of shoved me back a little and turned me to the side, but it didn't knock me down, and it didn't hurt.

Still, I missed the can.

Grampa let me load and shoot his gun about five more times. I only hit the can once, and that was an accident.

After that, we headed off toward the house. I walked beside Grampa, carrying the gun so that it was pointed in a safe direction.

"Can we practice some more tomorrow?" I asked.

Grampa lit his pipe.

"Your shoulder's gonna be a mite sore for a couple of days," he said. "Let's wait till Saturday."

My shoulder didn't hurt, but I could tell it was going to be a little sore.

"Think I'll be ready to shoot rats Saturday?"

When Grampa smiled, his pipe stuck straight out.

"Get to where I'm sure you can handle the gun safely and where you can hit four cans in a row." He grinned. "Then we'll go for the rats."

"Saturday, for sure." I smiled. "I'll hit four cans in a row. I can do it now."

CHAPTER 12

"I finally got that stinkin' rat this morning," I told Beauty. "Figured I'd be able to do it sooner, only it took me a whole week of practice. I had to hit the four cans before Grampa would let me go after that rat."

Beauty chomped a mouthful of grass.

"I guess I got him with the first shot, but I wasn't sure, so I shot again. When I did, I . . . ah . . . I knocked kind of a little hole in Grampa's barn. I figured he was gonna kill me, or at least yell at me, but he just laughed. Can you imagine? He laughed, out loud even. He said, 'That happens to the best of us.' Then he showed me where he had accidentally shot some holes in the barn, and he let me help patch the one I made."

Beauty was almost next to my ear. I rolled my head. It was strange looking right up at the huge white horse who was nearly standing on top of me. I wasn't worried, though. I knew Beauty wouldn't step on me, not even accidentally. Still, I kept an eye on her.

She moved a couple of feet away to graze on some clover. I laced my fingers behind my head and yawned.

It was noon, and even under the huge cottonwood trees where I was lying, the sun beat down, almost cutting straight through the leaves. The breeze that rippled the pool was soft. It made the hot noonday sun feel almost cool on my body.

The birds were quiet, except for the mockingbird who sang his song from some place in the big tree. He was on the other side from where I lay, and I couldn't see him. But I could still hear the loud, bragging song that told his sweetheart how handsome and strong he was.

It felt good, lying here with nothing on. The wind seemed to touch every bit of me. The grass felt soft and cool on my back. I closed my eyes and let the wind tickle my skin.

"I'm getting where I kinda like my grampa," I told

Beauty, looking in the tree for that noisy mocking-bird. "He's loud and gruff sometimes, but we really had fun learning to shoot his old gun."

I raised up on one elbow. Beauty had moved around to the other side of where I lay. She was grazing between me and the pool. That clear blue water sure looked cool and fresh.

"I like Mike, too. You know, the first week I took those riding lessons, I thought it was boring. I've learned a lot, though. Besides that, I got to meet Joshua.

"He's coming out later. His folks have a horse trailer, and you and I are going to ride with him and his horse. I don't think I'll show him our pool. Not yet, anyway. This is our private place. It's just for you and me."

Beauty had wandered to the edge of the water. She pawed it with one hoof. Water splashed everywhere. Then she changed feet and pawed with the other. She seemed to be playing and having a good time, like a little kid in the bathtub.

Some of the water she was splashing hit me. It felt just as cool as I knew it would. I got up and went into the pond beside her.

She leaned down to get a drink. Then she nuzzled my bare stomach, and I patted her forehead. Although she was all white, there was an even whiter spot right in the middle of her forehead. It was in the shape of a little star.

"Well," I said, looking at the water, "since you're through playing and since I'm already wet, might as well swim some. Then we got to get back to the barn to meet Joshua."

Joshua came about 1:30. I already had Beauty saddled and ready to go. Joshua's folks stayed around while we saddled his horse Rambo. They visited with Mama and Grampa; then, when they saw us riding up, they went to their truck.

"We'll be back around six or so," Joshua's dad called. "You boys be careful."

Joshua nodded and waved. "We will."

They drove away, Grampa and Mama went back into the house, and we headed off to the east pasture. To me, that was the best place to ride. It had hills and creeks and canyons, where the cows grazed, and all sorts of neat trails through the blackjack trees. There was lots of stuff to explore, too.

We talked about a bunch of things as we rode. I was mainly interested in school. Joshua told me about all of the teachers we would have next year. He explained who the mean ones were and who to look out for; who was fun and who was good and who wasn't very good; who you could learn stuff from and who just wanted to pass the time and get the day over with. He said the principal wasn't very strict and that she let them get away with lots of stuff. He said he liked that, kind of, but sometimes it wasn't much fun for everybody to be acting wild. He *didn't* like that.

After talking about school he told me about the football game he had planned for Tuesday when I got to go to town. He told me the names of the guys who were going to be there and what they were like and about how neat they were.

We explored two creeks and one stand of blackjack trees. He asked all sorts of stuff: what my school was like, and what it was like living in a big city instead of a little town like Chickasha, and who my friends were, and what it was like to move—since he'd lived in the same place all his life and his family never moved. Then he asked about my daddy.

I didn't tell him much—only that Daddy had left us a couple of years ago because he and Mama couldn't get along, or didn't love each other any more, or something.

I didn't tell him the important stuff. Like how Daddy was always promising to do things with me, only he never showed up. Or how he promised to take me on the Morning Trail and never came. Or how he promised to write, and I hadn't heard from him in over a year and a half. I didn't tell him how my stomach used to hurt or how I cried, night after night, when I'd hear Mama and Daddy screaming at each other in the other room. I didn't tell him any of that.

That sort of thing is something you can only tell your *best* friend. Without thinking, I reached down and patted Beauty on the neck.

"Fact is, you're the only one I've ever told stuff like that to," I thought out loud.

"What?" Joshua asked.

I jumped and turned in my saddle so I could look back at him.

"Oh, nothing," I said, feeling my face get all hot. "I was just talking to myself."

His eyes flashed.

"Hey, look over there." He pointed up the trail. "Those your grampa's cows?"

I turned to see where he was pointing. Before I could even answer, he went galloping around me and raced off up the trail.

"Come on," he called. "Let's play cowboys!"

I kicked Beauty in the sides and raced after him.

"Hey, wait a minute," I called.

It was no use. Joshua and Rambo went flying right

through the middle of Grampa's cattle. The cows snorted at them, then they scattered in every direction. One cow knocked her baby down, trying to move out of Rambo's way. She didn't even stop to see if it was all right.

The calf rolled clear over on its side. Quickly, it scrambled to its feet, looked around, and its tail went straight up in the air as it raced off after its mama.

Joshua kept running Rambo as hard and fast as he could. I kept chasing after him, yelling "Wait! Stop!"

Finally, after Joshua had scattered all the cows into the blackjacks, he pulled Rambo to a stop. Rambo was breathing hard but pawing the ground to go again when I caught up with them.

"Grampa's told me not to run his cows," I told him. "We'll get in trouble if—"

"How's he gonna know?" Joshua cut me off. "We're clear across the pasture from the house. Nobody can see us. Come on. Let's round them up."

I waved at a gnat buzzing in my face. "I . . . I don't know. What if . . ."

"Come on. We'll get them back in a circle here in the middle, then move them over to that next bunch of blackjacks."

"I . . . I don't know . . ." I stammered.

"We can make like it's a real cattle drive. You know, 'Get along little dogie' and all that stuff. Let's get 'em."

Joshua and Rambo took off again. He pointed to the right as he rode away.

"You get that bunch over there."

I sat for a moment, then pulled Beauty's reins to the right. "Maybe he's right. Who's gonna know? It might be fun."

It *was* fun!

It took us a long time to get the cows gathered back in the opening near the middle of the trees. We snuck around behind them and moved two or three at a time, then circled back for others. We dodged tree limbs and yelled and shouted and whooped it up, just like in the movies. When we had all the cows together, we moved them slowly down the path.

"You ever see the movie *Cowboys?*" Joshua asked.

"The one with John Wayne?"

"Yeah."

He waved his arms to keep the cows moving down the trail. "I bet if we lived back then," he said, waving his arms again, "I bet we could make it as real cowboys. I bet we could go on a trail drive and eat around a chuck wagon and sleep out under the stars."

"Yeah," I added, "and carry a six-shooter and a lariat and . . ."

"And fight off Indians and outlaws," Joshua chimed in. "And . . ."

I took it up. "And go to a saloon and drink whiskey and play cards and get in fights."

We both laughed. We rode quietly, dreaming about being real cowboys and what things were like in the old days and what heroes we would have been.

The cows stayed together down the path through the blackjacks. We moved them slowly. We watched them swat at the big gray flies with their tails. We looked at the soft cloud of dust kicked up by their hoofs.

When we got to the edge of the trees, the cows started to spread out. Suddenly, Joshua looked behind us.

"Indians," he screamed. "Head for the fort."

He kicked Rambo in the sides, so hard the horse almost shot out from under him. I kicked Beauty too.

The cows raced ahead of us. They had their tails up. They glanced back every now and then to see how close we were. We waved our arms, yelling and hollering as we chased them across the top of the hill and to the safety of the blackjack fort ahead of us.

Right as we topped the hill, Beauty stumbled. She

didn't go down, but we were running so fast when she tripped, I almost fell out of the saddle. I grabbed the horn and slipped over to the side. I had to fight to get myself back up.

She started to trot, but I pulled on the reins. I made her walk. For a minute I thought she was limping. But I looked down and couldn't see anything wrong with her leg, so we took off again after Joshua.

Beauty could run like the wind! It wasn't until after the cows had disappeared into the safety of the blackjack trees and we turned and started walking toward home that I noticed Beauty limping. She was breathing so hard I could hear the puffing sound. I could feel her sides heaving in and out under my legs.

Every time she put weight on her right foreleg, she jarred me in the saddle.

"It's almost dark," Joshua said. "I bet my folks are already at your house. Let's go."

He kicked Rambo to a trot. Beauty wasn't limping so much anymore, so I made her trot too. When she trotted, I didn't notice any limp at all.

"That was fun," Joshua said when I got off Beauty to open the gate. "Hope Dad's not too mad at me for being late. Maybe he'll let me come back, and we can do it again. I can't tell from here whether he looks mad or not. Can you?"

I closed the gate and looked toward the house.

Joshua's dad was sitting on the fender of his pickup. He had his arms folded and was watching us.

Beauty was still breathing hard. She wasn't puffing as bad as when we finished chasing the cows, though. I climbed back on her after I closed the gate.

"I can't tell either."

Joshua leaned close to me. "I'll see if he'll let me come again," he whispered. "I can usually talk him into stuff. We'll play cowboys. That is," he cautioned, "as long as nobody knows. Right?"

I smiled. "Right."

The only trouble was, Grampa knew!

CHAPTER 13

How he knew I'm not sure. But he knew.

I could tell by the way his eyes tightened up and the smoke from his old black pipe rolled in thick clouds over the top of his head. He didn't say anything. He just looked at me and looked at Beauty and didn't say a word. Not until Joshua and his dad drove off.

When their horse trailer bounced and rattled across the cattle guard at the bottom of the drive, Grampa turned to me.

I wanted to hold my ears. I braced myself for the yelling and roaring that I knew was coming. Instead, his voice was really soft. "There are some cloth feed sacks beside the grain bin. Find a clean one, shake out the dust, and wipe her down."

He reached over and dragged his fingers across Beauty's chest. I hadn't noticed how lathered up she was. There were little ringlets of foamy-looking sweat all over her chest and shoulders. Grampa walked around her. When he got beside her right foreleg, he stopped.

"You fall?"

I followed his eyes to Beauty's knee. It seemed a little bigger than the knee on her left foreleg. I swallowed the knot in my throat and shook my head.

"No sir. She tripped, but she didn't fall. She didn't even limp. Well . . . not much."

He looked up at me. His eyes cut right through me. Then he turned and went to the house.

I almost had all the sweat off Beauty by the time Grampa came to the barn. He had two big Ziploc bags filled with ice. Holding them in one hand, he inspected Beauty's leg again. He rubbed it and made her lift her foot. Then he rubbed her knee some more.

"Sprained knee, I think." His voice was still soft. "How did it happen?"

I swallowed.

"She tripped."

His eyes got tighter, but his voice got softer. "I

know that. But how? What were you doing?"

I wanted to lie. I wanted to tell him we were just walking along and she tripped, and I didn't know . . . But I looked at his tight eyes and thought about how soft his voice was, and instead of lying, I told him everything!

Grampa listened, and when I was finished, he didn't say a word. He just nodded his head. Finally, he handed me the bags with the ice.

"Hold these on the knee till most of the ice is melted. Probably help some. Tomorrow morning we'll do it again."

I held the ice bags on both sides of Beauty's knee. I couldn't look up at Grampa.

"I'm sorry. I'll never do it again. Promise. I didn't mean to hurt her. I don't think any of the cows are hurt. They acted okay. I'm sorry I ran them. I know you told me not to. I'm sorry I didn't mind you. I don't know why. I'm sorry—"

I stopped, feeling the tears creep into the corners of my eyes. No matter what, I wasn't going to cry in front of Grampa.

"It isn't the cows," he said from behind me. "Shoot, I'm not worried about the cows. Little running don't hurt them a bit. It's this old horse."

He leaned forward and patted her neck. I looked

down at the ground so he wouldn't see the little tear that squeezed out of my eye.

"She's an *old* lady, Luke. She's old and tired and stiff—just like I am. She's past the age for running and herding cattle."

"I'm sorry." I sniffed back the tears, hoping Grampa hadn't heard me.

He put a hand on my shoulder. "Ain't your fault, boy."

I wiped my cheek with the sleeve of my shirt and turned to look up at him. "It is too!"

Grampa only smiled and shook his head. "Not really. Boy gets on a horse, he's got to ride. Got to kick up his heels and go tearing across the pasture and got to let his imagination go running free and wild. That's only natural." He kind of punched my shoulder. "I know how boys are. I used to be one."

He knelt beside me. He put his hands on top of mine and scooted the ice packs to the sides of Beauty's knee.

"Anyhow, boys got to do stuff like that. If you didn't, I'd worry about you, 'cause, like I said, it's natural. I was just hoping you could hold off till we got you used to Lady. She's a lot younger and in better shape. Now, *she's* a boy's horse."

I frowned, tilting my head to the side.

"That's why you want me to ride her? Why you want me to take lessons at Mike's?"

Grampa smiled. "She'll carry you all day if you want to ride that long. She can keep up with a boy and then still have some left." He reached up and patted Beauty's neck again. "This old gal . . . Well, she's a great horse. Perfect for kids or somebody who doesn't know how to ride. But she's old. Real old. She's earned her way in this world. Worked hard and honest all her life. Now, though, she's getting like me. She probably doesn't have much time left, and what there is, she deserves to spend easy and quiet. Understand?"

I nodded, but I couldn't say anything.

Grampa knelt beside me for a long time. He made a grunting sound as he got to his feet. I held the ice bags to Beauty's foreleg. I squeezed my eyes shut.

Grampa reached down and ruffled my hair. "It's okay, boy. She'll be fine. And you'll learn to ride Lady, like you need to."

He turned. I could hear him shuffling across the barn. "I'll have your mom hold supper for us till you get in," he called.

When he'd gone, I opened my eyes and looked up at Beauty.

"I'm sorry," I told her. "I didn't mean to hurt you." I wiped my cheek on my shirt sleeve. "I understand what Grampa said and why he wants me to ride Lady. But you're my horse now. I love you. No matter what, I won't leave you. I'll help you get better, and I'll take care of you and I won't ever make you run or chase cows—never. I love you and I won't ever leave you. That's a promise."

CHAPTER 14

The ice packs didn't seem to do much good. The next morning, Beauty's right knee looked twice as big as the other one. I went to the house and fixed the ice for her myself. At noon I put ice on her leg again.

Grampa reminded me that Mike was going to work with me and Lady. Classes were over, but he wanted me to come at the regular time so he could make sure I was ready to handle her. I walked over.

Mike had me ride Lady in the indoor arena, just like during the regular class, only instead of having me go slow and easy, he made me gallop and make a lot more turns and even stop and back up.

When I was getting ready to leave, he came over and put one of his huge hands on my shoulder.

"Done good, Luke." He smiled. "Tomorrow we'll let you try her in the pasture. I've got her gentled and reining more than cutting. Still, riding in the open is different from riding inside. She's gonna act different around cattle. Think I'll bring some of the calves in here on Thursday, just to let you get the feel of her when she's working. A working cuttin' horse is a lot different from what you're used to. Still, she's a good horse and you're a darn good rider. Think you'll manage."

That kind of made my chest swell up. Then, remembering Beauty, I patted his arm and said thank you. I told him I'd see him tomorrow.

I was almost to the barbed wire fence at the edge of our place when I heard him calling from his barn. "Why don't you invite your mom to come watch tomorrow. She might enjoy seeing how much you've learned. Tuesday is her day off, isn't it?"

I nodded. "Think so. I'll ask her."

Mama was still at work when I got home, so I fixed more ice for Beauty and went to the barn. The leg looked about the same. At least it hadn't gotten any bigger, but it didn't look any better, either.

At supper I asked Mama if she'd like to come watch me ride Lady. She thought it over a while and shrugged.

"I guess. Do *you* want me to come?"

I smiled and nodded. "Yeah."

She frowned again and kind of tilted her head to the side. "I was planning to go to the grocery store tomorrow. Guess I could wait and get groceries when I take you to Joshua's. That would leave me time for Mr. Garrison's in the morning. Oh, by the way, do you know where Joshua lives?"

I shook my head. "No. But I got his phone number. I'll call and ask."

"Be sure and write down the address."

"I will."

After visiting with Joshua on the phone, I could hardly wait for tomorrow. There was a whole bunch of guys coming over to his house. It sounded like a great way to meet people and make new friends. I was so excited I had trouble getting to sleep. I tossed and turned and flipped and flopped. The next morning, I woke up a good hour before breakfast.

Since I was already up, I decided to go ahead and take care of Beauty. I got dressed, fixed the ice bags, and headed for the barn.

It surprised me when I went to open the gate and saw Grampa and Mike. They were kneeling down, looking at Beauty's leg.

All of a sudden the excitement about going to Joshua's drained out of me, like water draining out of a bathtub. A cold chill came to take its place.

There was something really wrong with my horse if Grampa had called Mike over. Maybe it couldn't be fixed. Maybe she wouldn't ever get well. Maybe I had hurt her so bad . . .

"She'll be okay," I heard Mike tell Grampa. "About a week or so, I figure. But the boy's gonna have to take it easy with her. At her age it's a wonder she's still up and around, much less able to carry a rider."

A sigh of relief whooshed out of my chest. My horse was all right.

Grampa must have heard me. He glanced up and smiled. "You're up early. Excited about the big football game today?"

Nodding my head, I smiled back. Mike waved a huge hand. "Came over to see how the old gal's feed supply was holding out. Your grampa wanted me to take a look at her leg. Think she's gonna be fine."

My smile got even bigger.

Mike stood and walked over to the feed sacks stacked against the side of the barn.

"Five sacks left, Willie. Want about another ton?"

Grampa stuck his pipe in his mouth, but he didn't light it. "Ton will probably do her awhile," Grampa answered. "How many bales of alfalfa you need?"

Mike stroked his beard.

"Willie, I'll probably need ten. Twelve. Something

like that. I got plenty of oats to mix in, but we'll have to buy the bran. You want molasses mixed in, too?"

Grampa nodded. "Sure. You know what a sweet tooth the old gal has."

Mike was on the other side of Grampa. They stopped talking about Beauty's food, and Mike looked around Grampa at me.

"What ya' got, Luke?"

"Ice packs for her leg," I answered.

They both came over to where I was. Mike knelt down beside me.

"When did she twist it?"

"Sunday."

"Ice won't help much. Not now. Come on out to the truck with me. I got some stuff that might help her."

I handed the ice bags to Grampa and followed Mike. He dug around in the big toolbox in the back of his truck and pulled out a plastic can that said Dream Whip on the label. Then he hunted around some more until he found a paint brush, about as wide as my hand.

My nose crinkled. "I didn't know Dream Whip was good for horses."

He laughed with that big, booming roar of his. "Not dairy topping," he said, shaking his head. "Liniment. It's called D.M.S.O. It's good stuff. It'll help ease her knee. But you put it on with a brush. Don't want to get it on your hands."

"Why not?"

"Well," Mike said, motioning me to follow him. "It absorbs almost instantly through the skin and into the system. It's not poisonous or bad for you or anything. It's just for animals, though. Not people. Besides"—he made a spitting sound—"it tastes like raw oysters. Spilled some on my foot one time while I was putting it in a different container. Tasted like I'd been eating raw oysters for two days. Nasty." He made the spitting sound again.

Mike showed me how to paint the D.M.S.O. on Beauty's leg. Then we found a place to store the stuff and wrapped the brush in a paper towel. Grampa invited Mike in for coffee, and we headed for the house.

Grampa already had the coffee on. He poured Mike a cup, then one for himself.

They talked some more about Beauty's feed. Grampa said he was going to cut hay Thursday and then windrow it (whatever that means), and it would probably be ready and baled by Sunday or Monday if his baler worked.

"You still got that old hay baler?" Mike scoffed.

A puff of smoke rolled up Grampa's forehead. "Can't afford a new one. Too high."

Mike shook his head. "Thing's as old as you are, Willie. You spend more time kicking and cussing at it than you do baling hay. Be cheaper in the long run and a whole lot safer if you'd get a new one. You can borrow mine if you want."

Grampa shrugged.

"Nope. The one I've got will still do the job."

Mike looked over the top of his coffee cup at me and cocked his eyebrows.

"You know, Luke, that old hay baler is just about as stubborn and cantankerous as your grampa. That thing's gonna be the death of him yet. I mean, if he doesn't quit—"

Mike stopped in the middle of his sentence because right then Mama came in. She was still half asleep. She'd just put her hair up in hot rollers and had on her little pink shorty nightgown.

She yawned as she got to the kitchen and was halfway to the table before she saw us sitting there.

All of a sudden her eyes popped wide and her mouth fell open. She covered her chest with her arms. Then, realizing her legs were sticking out, she dropped her hands there. Then she crossed them over her chest again.

Finally, like she couldn't decide what to cover up, she put one hand down at her legs and the other over her chest. She squealed, spun around, and raced back down the hall.

We all sat there for a second with our mouths open. Finally, Grampa cleared his throat.

"Guess I should have let her know we had company. Wasn't expecting her up this early, not on her day off."

Mike didn't say anything. He just looked down at his coffee cup.

"She doesn't like anybody seeing her without her hair done or without her makeup on," I said, remembering how Mama wouldn't even run to the convenience store in Denver with her hair mussed. "She's kinda funny about stuff like that."

Mike still didn't say anything. He took a big drink of his coffee. When he set his cup down, he nudged me with an elbow.

"Don't tell your mom I said so, but even with her hair messed up she's a mighty attractive young lady."

I smiled. Grampa chuckled. Mike finished his coffee and said he'd best be getting back to work. I wanted to ask him what he was fixing to say about Grampa's hay baler and about "it being the death of him," but I forgot.

CHAPTER 15

Mama didn't go with me for my lesson with Mike Garrison. She said she had something she needed to do at home. She did pick me up when it was time to go to Joshua's, though, but instead of coming in she just sat in the car and honked the horn.

Mike walked with me to the door.

"Go on," he said. "I'll unsaddle Lady for you." He looked out the barn door and waved to Mama, but she didn't wave back. He looked down and kicked at the dirt with his boots.

"Tell your mom I said 'hi'."

"Okay," I called over my shoulder as I raced toward the car and my football game. "See you tomorrow."

* * *

The football game was great. There were five other guys there besides Joshua and me. Since we didn't divide up even, Joshua was quarterback for both teams. That way there were four on a team.

Everybody was nice, and we had a lot of fun. Nobody got mean or lost his temper or tried to show off. We just played. When we got tired, Joshua's mom brought some Kool-Aid out, and we sat around and talked.

The best thing was that we planned to play again, Saturday noon. Once we decided that, we changed around our teams, so different people could cover each other, and we played some more.

"You have fun?" Mama asked when I climbed in the car.

"Sure did. We're gonna play again Saturday. Can you bring me to town?"

"No, I've got to work, but I'm sure your grandfather can. We'll ask him when we get home. Did you make some new friends?"

I got up on my knees to explore the grocery sacks in the back seat.

"I sure did," I answered. I found a box of fudge bars and got one out. "They're nice guys. Everybody except Jeff. He likes to show people how many bad words he knows. He only says 'em when he misses a pass." I kind of chuckled, remembering. "And he missed a bunch of passes."

"Was Joshua okay?"

I chomped a bite out of the fudge bar. It was so cold it hurt. I swallowed the bite and rubbed my tongue across my teeth.

"Yeah. The guys like him. He's really popular, I think. He introduced me to all the guys and told me stuff about each one. He's a great quarterback, too. I never saw anybody, besides a grown-up, who could throw the ball as far or straight as he can." I shook my head. "Man, I wish I could throw like that."

When we got home, I helped Mama carry in the groceries. Then I headed to the barn.

Even before I got there, I could hear Grampa. He was growling and yelling and using words I'd never heard him say before. I tilted my head to the side and listened.

Wonder who he's talking to? I thought with a frown.

I found him working on a big piece of farm machinery just inside the door to the barn. He kicked it once, then took a wrench and twisted something on the side. He kicked it again and cussed some more.

Deciding it was best to leave him alone, I went and got the medicine for Beauty. She stood really still while I painted the stuff on her leg. I fixed her a bucket of feed and told her all about the football game and about Joshua and all the fun I had. Finally, Grampa quit yelling at his machine. Pretty soon he came down to the end of the barn where I was.

"How long you been here, Luke?" he asked.

"About fifteen minutes."

His mouth kind of twitched up on one side. "You hear any of the discussion I was having with my hay baler?"

I squeezed my lips between my teeth and nodded.

Grampa's eyes rolled up to look at the ceiling, then back at me.

"Tell you what," he said, smiling. "You don't repeat any of those words I was calling the baler around your mom, and I'll . . ."

"Will you take me to town on Saturday? There's another football game."

His smile got even bigger. He poked his pipe in his mouth.

"I'll take you to town on Saturday."

"Promise?"

He put a finger to his lips, reminding me not to repeat anything he had said.

"I'll promise if you will."

"Promise," I answered.

Grampa motioned with a jerk of his head. "Come on. Let's get to the house."

I picked up the liniment and went to put it away. Then I went back to Beauty. She leaned her head down, and I scratched behind her ears, where she liked.

"Things are really looking up, Beauty. Your leg's getting better, and I really can ride Lady now." Then I leaned over and whispered in her ear. "But you're still my horse, and I'm not gonna ride that other horse unless I have to."

She nuzzled my chest as I scratched.

"Grampa's gonna take me to town Saturday. Mama's supposed to find out whether she gets a job permanently, instead of just when the other women are on vacation. I bet she does, don't you? And most important, Grampa's being nice to me. He doesn't yell near as much as he did when we first came here. He's not near as grumpy. I like him now."

But by the time I got to the house, Grampa was grumpy again.

Grampa and Mama were yelling at each other. I stood at the door a minute before I went in. I didn't like the yelling. It reminded me of back in Denver, before Daddy left.

I couldn't really make out all they were hollering about. Somebody had called Mama on the phone and asked her to go someplace. Mama had said no, and

Grampa was upset about it. Leastways, that's the best I could make out from all the yelling.

Finally I got up the nerve to go in. I walked over and sat down in the big chair across from Mama. They both glanced at me, then went right on talking.

"He asked you last week to go to the show with him. And it's not like he's asking you out to a bar to get drunk or something," Grampa fussed. "It's a church social, for gosh sakes. I mean, what's wrong with that?"

Mama folded her arms. "I just don't want to."

"Why not? There will be a Wednesday evening service. Then afterwards there'll be a whole bunch of people for ice cream and cake. And then—"

"I don't feel like going," Mama answered in a really snippy voice.

Grampa didn't mind cutting people off by interrupting in the middle of something they were saying. But when somebody interrupted what he was saying, he didn't like it a bit.

The smoke really rolled up out of that old black pipe of his. He bit down on it so hard, I thought I could hear his teeth grinding.

"Fine! Got your fingers burned once, so you ain't even gonna get close to the stove—ever again. Right?"

Mama didn't answer.

I frowned, since I didn't have any idea what he was talking about. Stove? Getting burned? I couldn't remember Mama getting burned while she was cooking anything—not lately, anyhow.

Grampa's eyes got really narrow when he looked down at Mama. "You might as well pitch in the towel, Carol." He looked mad, but he spoke soft and gentle. "If you're that scared of life and living, you might as well just give up."

Mama glared back at him. Her voice wasn't nearly as soft or gentle.

"I'm not scared! I'm just not ready to start dating again."

"It's been two years. How long's it gonna take?"

Mama's answer was really snotty. "When I want to start dating, I'll decide. I'll let you know."

I figured Grampa would get mad again, since she was sassing him, only he didn't. He put his pipe down in the ashtray and took a deep breath.

"I know it hurt, Carol. I know it hurt something terrible when Jerry left you and Luke. But you can't let the hurt destroy you. When life kicks you in the teeth like that, you can't draw into your shell and hide. You got to keep going. You got to live with the hurt for a while. Then you got to let the hurt go away and start living again.

"Don't let Jerry destroy you. He's not worth it. He proved that when he left. He just ain't worth it."

I saw a tear roll down Mama's cheek, only I couldn't tell if it was a mad tear or a sad tear.

"He didn't destroy me," she said. "It's just . . . I'm not ready . . . I don't want—"

"You don't want to take any chances." Grampa finished Mama's stammering for her. "You don't want to take a chance on dating or trusting or falling in love 'cause you figure you're leaving yourself open to the hurt again, if you ever do.

"Like I said, Carol, if you're too scared to trust or to love, you might as well quit living altogether. You can't go through this world without trusting or loving. That ain't living."

Mama got up off the couch. I could see the tears streaming down her cheeks.

"Good night." She sniffed. "I'm going to bed."

And she left.

Grampa only shook his head. "It's getting late," he told me with a shrug of his big shoulders. "Guess we could all use a good night's sleep."

I stood in the living room by myself for a few minutes. Grown-up talk was sure confusing sometimes. I didn't know what was going on. I *did* know that my mama was crying, and it was Grampa who made her cry. I wanted to tell Grampa how I felt and how he shouldn't be so grumpy, even if he was trying to help. But I figured, What's the use?

I headed for my bedroom. "Talking to Grampa is like trying to talk to a grizzly bear. All he does is growl. Tomorrow I'll talk it over with Beauty. She's the only one around here I can really talk to, the only one I can really trust."

CHAPTER 16

"It's probably somebody she met at work," I told Beauty as I painted the medicine on the inside of her knee.

The swelling seemed to be going down. Her knee wasn't nearly as big as yesterday.

"Maybe it's somebody she doesn't even like. Grampa wants her to go to this church thing, and she doesn't want to go. She ought to be the one to decide. I mean if this guy is a jerk or something . . . Why would she want to go out with a jerk?"

I finished painting on the medicine and got to my feet. Beauty lowered her head, resting it against my chest so I would rub her ears.

"He was saying stuff about Daddy, too. He

shouldn't do that. I mean, Daddy was okay. He used to do all sorts of stuff with us. He'd take us places and laugh and have fun and . . . and . . ."

I stood quietly for a long time, remembering. I thought about all the times that Daddy had promised things. Only the things he promised never happened.

I don't know how long I stood there, dreaming. Beauty shoved me with her nose. She still wanted her ears scratched.

"It's a lie," I told her, starting to scratch again. "The things I told you, they really weren't true. Daddy hardly ever took us places. He said he was going to—a trip to Disney World, a plane to Hawaii—all sorts of neat stuff. Only he always had to work.

"Even little things, like going to the show or out to eat—that never happened either. You know what happened on my birthday two years ago?"

Her ears twitched forward.

"I'll tell you what happened. He promised to take me to Elitches Amusement Park, you know, for all the rides and stuff like that. When he came home, his breath smelled funny."

I stopped scratching her ears to scratch my nose. She nuzzled me again.

"Mama said the funny smell was booze but not to say anything to Daddy about it. Anyway, he came home, and I asked him if he was ready to take me to the amusement park. He just grunted and told me to forget it. Then he went in and plopped down on his bed and didn't wake up till the next morning. Mama said something to him about taking me that day, since he missed my birthday. He griped about how bad his head hurt and told her to shut up. It started another big fight. Seems like that's all Daddy did was yell at Mama and want to fight.

"He did take me riding in Aspen. Took me on the Morning Trail." I swallowed the knot in my throat and shook my head. "That sure seems like a long time ago."

I quit scratching her ears and closed the gate behind me as I left her pasture. I crossed my arms over the top rail of the fence, resting my chin on them.

"He called, once. Promised me he was gonna take me on the Morning Trail. Then, the day he was supposed to come, he called and said he had something else he had to do, but we would go next year. But the next year he never even called, Beauty. He just doesn't care."

Beauty had backed up to the big corner post, next to the gate. She pushed her tail against it and started rubbing back and forth. When she got that silly look on her face, when her bottom lip started flopping up and down, it made me smile.

* * *

Grampa was talking on the phone when I got inside for breakfast. He turned to Mama.

"That's Mike," he told her. "He apologized. Said calling you Tuesday to invite you out Wednesday really wasn't enough notice. He said if you'd reconsider, he'd bake the cake and fix the ice cream. All you'd have to do is ride to church with him."

I had no idea it was Mike that had called Mama! I figured it was some dumb guy she'd met at work or in town. But Mike!

Mama stood staring at Grampa. She set the plate of scrambled eggs down on the table, never once taking her icy stare off him. I rushed over beside her and tugged at her sleeve. She didn't look at me. I tugged again.

"Mama . . ."

Grampa shrugged and held the phone out to her. Mama just kept staring at him.

I tugged on her sleeve again. "Mama . . ."

Finally she turned to look at me.

I smiled. "Mama. Mike's really nice. I like him."

She glared at me the way she had at Grampa. Then, slowly, the mean look left her face. She gave a big sigh, and her shoulders kind of slumped. My smile got even bigger. She looked back at Grampa. Slowly, almost like she hated to do it, Mama nodded her head.

Before she had time to change her mind, Grampa yanked the phone to his ear.

"She'd be thrilled, Mike. Can hardly wait. What time?"

Grampa nodded. "Six o'clock. She'll be ready."

Mama's mouth flopped open. Before she could close it, Grampa hung up the phone.

Mama finally got her mouth shut. She went to the stove and took the bacon off the skillet. When she put the plate down, it banged so hard, I thought it was going to break. Then she got glasses for the orange juice and put them in front of where Grampa and I were sitting. She banged them on the table too.

Finally, she plopped herself in her chair. She sat with such a thud, I thought she was going to bust the chair legs.

Grampa never looked up. Mama took a drink of her juice. She folded her arms and glared at him, then at me.

"You know, the only reason I'm going is to shut you two up."

Grampa took a bite of his eggs. I played around with mine and without glancing up took a bite of bacon.

"I probably won't have a good time."

Grampa kept his head down, but he raised his eyebrows and wiggled them at me.

"There will probably just be a bunch of old folks there. Nobody knows me. Nobody will probably even talk to me."

Grampa winked at me. My smile was so big, a piece of bacon dropped out of my mouth. I clamped my lips shut.

"Besides, I don't even know what I'm supposed to wear." She got up from the table and went to prowl around in her room. "Go to work all day, come home, then have to get dressed again to go with some dumb cowboy to some dumb church social. Don't even have anything to wear."

She kept muttering all the way down the hall. Finally, when we couldn't hear her voice anymore, Grampa looked up. His smile stretched clear across his wrinkled face.

"I'm glad she's gonna go with him," I said.

Grampa's smile softened, but his eyes seemed to dance.

"Me too. Mike's a good man. A darned good man."

The riding lesson was fun that afternoon. I never even got on Lady, but it was fun anyway.

As soon as I got there and we saddled her, Mike started asking me all sorts of stuff about Mama. He wanted to know what she liked and what she didn't like, what kind of things she enjoyed talking about, what her favorite TV show was, what colors she liked. Did she like flowers? Did she like chocolate cake better than lemon? He asked everything you could imagine, and then some.

A man came and yelled at Mike that he was ready to pick up the horse he'd bought last week. Mike looked at his watch.

"We missed your lesson," he told me. "Sorry."

I smiled up at him. "No problem. Hope you and Mama have a good time."

He reached out and ruffled my hair. His hand was so huge, it covered the whole top of my head.

"Tell you what. Anytime you want, you come over and we'll ride. Lesson's on me."

He ran across the arena to go visit with the guy. I almost laughed out loud to myself. It looked more like he was skipping than running.

I finished painting the medicine on Beauty's leg.

"I sure hope they have a good time tonight. I hope Mama doesn't get snotty like she did with Grampa. I bet if they have a good time, if Mama will just give Mike half a chance, she'll like him as much as I do."

Beauty flopped her ears. I petted her and took off for the house.

CHAPTER 17

Grampa and I turned the lights out in the living room. When we heard them drive up, both of us rushed to the window and peeked out.

Mama was laughing and giggling. Mike got out and walked her to the porch. Grampa and I held our breath, listening.

They stood there on the porch, talking and visiting for a long time. Then Mike said, "Oh, I almost forgot."

He trotted out to his truck and came back with a small cylinder thing with a lid on it. "Saved this for Willie and Luke. Thought they might like some ice cream." He handed the container to Mama.

"How did you manage to save it? Those people

swarmed around that ice cream of yours like bees swarming honey."

I could hear Mike chuckle. "Snuck it out before they started serving it. Here."

"I had a wonderful time," Mama said. Then she opened the container of ice cream and looked in. "Daddy and Luke will enjoy this. Shame there's not any cake left to go with it." She smiled up at him.

Mike put his hands in his pockets and kind of shuffled his feet.

"I could make another. Bring it over."

Mama reached out and touched his big arm. "That would be nice. But only if you'd stay and eat it with us. Tomorrow evening? Around seven?"

Mike cleared his throat and nodded. "I'll be here."

They shook hands, and Mama reached for the doorknob. Grampa slugged me on the shoulder. He motioned with a jerk of his head.

Quiet as a couple of rats in the barn, we raced across the living room. We landed in our chairs in the kitchen like a major league ball player sliding into home plate. Grampa grabbed his newspaper and rocked back in his chair. I had to slap a hand over my mouth to keep from laughing out loud. Still, I couldn't help the little snort and giggle that snuck out.

"You got it upside down," I laughed.

Grampa flipped the paper over. He shot me a real mean look. I got quiet.

Mama came in and put the ice cream in the freezer. Grampa looked over the top of his paper.

"Have a nice time, Carol?"

Mama smiled, then she got kind of a strange look on her face as she stared at us.

"Yes," she admitted, still looking us over. "It was all right."

"What do you have there?" I asked. Then I clamped my lips shut so I wouldn't giggle.

Mama frowned. "Ice cream."

Grampa hid his face behind the paper. "No cake to go with it?"

Mama folded her arms and glared at both of us. I had to look away. She slammed the freezer door.

"You two sneaks been listening at the door?"

Grampa buried his face deeper in the paper. I almost fell out of my chair when I reached down to pretend I was tying my tennis shoe.

"Since you two are so interested, and *since* you haven't been listening and *don't* know what's going on, I'll tell you." She tried to make her voice sound mad. I could tell she really wasn't, though. "Mike is going to fix another cake and bring it over tomorrow evening." Then, putting her hands on her hips, she said, "Now, if there are no more questions, I'm going to bed. Some of us *do* have to work in the morning."

She whirled around and headed down the hall. Then she said, almost like she was talking to herself, "How anybody that big and rough-looking can make a cake that light and delicate . . ."

Grampa's smile popped up over the top of his paper. I smiled too.

Mama liked Mike!

Mike liked Mama, too.

I found that out the next morning when I went over to Mike's. It was too early for my lesson, but I couldn't stand it, so I went over as soon as I finished doctoring Beauty's leg.

Mike was feeding his horses. I found him by the grain bin with about twenty feed buckets surrounding him.

"Hi, Mike," I greeted. "Ready for my riding lesson?"

He looked startled as he stood up from the feed bin. But when he saw it was me, he smiled.

"Morning, Luke." Then he stroked his beard, real thoughtfully.

I could tell he was busy. I knew he was trying to figure out some excuse to go riding another time instead of now.

"I can come back this afternoon," I said.

Mike smiled and shook his head. "I promised you —any time, right?"

I shrugged. "That's okay. I can wait."

"Nope. Got to feed the horses first. You can help me. A promise is a promise."

That really surprised me. I don't guess I'd ever known anybody who made a promise and then *really* kept it. Not till now.

We fed the horses. Mike filled the buckets, and I helped him carry them and hang them on the hooks inside the horse stalls. We fed all of them except Lady and the little white mare I'd seen when I started taking riding lessons. Those were the two we were going to ride, and Mike said we'd feed them when we got back.

I brushed and saddled Lady, then waited for Mike in the arena. He led the little white horse in. She was wearing an old crusty-looking saddle, and the reins were big lengths of heavy rope instead of leather.

"Give me a minute or two before we take off," Mike called from the middle of the arena. "She's still green, and I need to get some of the bounce out of her before we go."

He climbed on her and kicked her in the side. Her ears lay flat back against her neck. She reared a little, then bucked a couple of times. After that she started walking.

When Mike wanted to turn her, instead of laying the reins against the side of her neck like I did with Lady or Beauty, he held one of the rope reins way out from the side of her head and pulled on it. She was really slow to turn. And every once in a while, she'd bounce and buck.

At last he rode over to where I was. She still had her ears laid back.

"Not a very good horse," I said, reaching out to pat her nose. "She bucks and stumbles and rears up. She's hard to turn, too, isn't she?"

Mike smiled and shook his head. "She's gonna be a fabulous horse. She's still a baby. Just turned two. Got some rough edges yet. But she's got the heart. The spirit. Gonna be every bit the horse old Beauty is." He patted her on the neck. "Yep. Gonna be just like her old grandmother."

I felt myself jerk. I had no idea. Then I remembered the first day I'd seen her, whinnying and jumping around in her pen, Mike had told me this was Lady's baby. He also said something about how she was colored like her grandmother. And since Lady was Beauty's baby . . . I shrugged and shook my head. I wondered why I hadn't figured it out before now.

Mike gave some last-minute instructions as we headed out of the barn. He told me stuff about keeping a tight rein on Lady if his horse got to bucking or rearing up. And if he got thrown, which he didn't think would happen, I was to get off Lady and hold her if the little white mare headed toward the barn.

Then we rode and had fun. Mostly we talked, about Mama and how nice Mike thought she was. Then we talked about the church social and how much more Mike liked that than some of the parties he went to back in New York City.

"You been to New York City?" I yelped. "I thought you were a cowboy. I didn't know cowboys—"

Mike's horse tried to turn around and head to the barn. He pulled hard on her rope rein and got her back beside Lady.

"Wasn't always a cowboy," he said, still struggling with his horse. "Used to be a tax consultant for a big Corporation. Too much politics. Too much being nice to people who weren't nice themselves. Too much suit and tie and parties and watching other people sneaking around stealing ideas from one another.

"Finally got fed up with it. Always loved horses, though. Always wanted my own place. By the way, did your mom *really* have a good time last night?"

I almost laughed, thinking how this made about

twenty times Mike had asked me that very same thing.

Instead of laughing, I smiled. "She *really* had a good time."

We had fun Thursday night. We played dominoes and ate ice cream and the cake Mike brought. It was really good, too—light and moist and downright delicious. We talked a bit and laughed a lot.

Grampa and I won the first game, and Mama and Mike won the second. When we finished playing, Mike offered to help Mama with the dishes. Grampa kicked me under the table.

"We're gonna go in the living room and watch TV."

I reached down and rubbed my shin. "Yeah. TV," I agreed, knowing that was the only way to keep from getting kicked again.

While they were doing dishes, Mike asked Mama to go out to eat and then to a picture show on Saturday night. Mama said yes.

Only they didn't get to go.

CHAPTER 18

Friday morning Beauty's knee looked a lot better. I knew it was still too sore for me to ride her, but I asked Grampa if I could lead her over to the pool and let her splash in the water.

He said the water would probably be good for her leg. Then he reminded me to be careful and to be sure and put the peroxide and alcohol in my ears when I got back.

Beauty and I splashed around in the pool. After a while she went to graze on the bank. I swam some, then lay down in the shade of the big tree.

"I think it's great that Mama and Mike are dating, don't you, Beauty?"

She chomped a mouthful of grass and swished at a fly with her tail.

"I mean, he's a neat guy. He knows everything there is to know about horses. And he must be smart, too, since he used to live in New York and was a kind of executive for a big company. Besides that . . ."

I stopped, remembering the piece of cake I'd swiped from the cupboard and wrapped in foil. I got up and went to where my pants were hanging on a willow limb. I unwrapped the cake and took a bite. Beauty walked over then, sniffing around to see what I was doing. I broke the rest of the cake in half and held it out to her with a flat hand. She gobbled it up. Her head bounced up and down as she ate.

When we finished the cake, I got dressed, put the halter on Beauty, and started for home.

"I think it would be great if they got married. Wouldn't it be something to have Mike for a daddy? It's probably way too early, though. They may not even like each other all that much. But maybe, just maybe . . ."

I was on the hill about a quarter of a mile from the barn when I heard someone yelling. I looked down to the valley below and saw Grampa with his tractor and the hay baler.

He was standing up on the thing, kicking at something. He was yelling at the top of his voice, cussing and generally telling the dumb machine *exactly* what he thought about it.

We watched him for a while. Finally, still cussing, he climbed back on the tractor. The hay started coming out of the back of the baler as he drove.

"Looks like poop coming out of the end of an earthworm, don't it, Beauty?"

She wiggled her ears.

"Yep," I answered for her. "That's what it looks like."

Grampa got in about suppertime that evening. He was still grumpy and muttering stuff under his breath about that dumb machine.

Joshua called right after we finished eating. There were about twice as many guys coming to his house for the football game tomorrow. His yard was big but not that big, so they decided to meet at the high school practice field out in Borden Park. I didn't know where Borden Park was, so he gave me directions and I wrote them down.

"You're a great pass receiver," he said. "You reckon your mom would let you play Mighty-Mite football when school starts? I'll talk to the coach and see if I can get you on my team."

"That'd be great," I yelped. Then, trying not to

sound *too* excited, I added, "I think I can talk her into it."

Saturday morning I woke up at four-thirty. I tossed and turned and finally made myself go back to sleep. But I got up again at six.

I put on my favorite Denver Broncos football shirt and my tennis shoes. I wasn't supposed to be there until ten. But I wanted to be ready.

Grampa was squirting oil on his hay baler when I went to doctor Beauty. He'd squirt, wiggle something, cuss, and then squirt again.

Beauty lowered her head and nuzzled my stomach when I stood up. After putting on the medicine I scratched her ears.

"Your leg looks almost well," I said, looking once more to see how much the swelling had gone down. "You're gonna be fine."

She wiggled her ears, and I kept scratching.

"You know, Joshua wants me to be on his football team. He must really think I'm good. He's even gonna talk to his coach about me.

"I got to eat a good breakfast. Got to be full of energy and in good shape for the game today. I don't want to mess up. If I do, he probably won't want me on his team anymore."

I patted her on the neck, put the liniment away,

and closed the gate behind me.

Mama left for work, and Grampa headed off to his hayfield. I caught him just before he started the tractor.

"Remember, you're gonna take me to town this morning?"

He frowned.

"The football game, Grampa. Remember?"

He nodded, but the frown stayed on his face. "I can't today, Luke. Got to get the hay in."

"But Grampa . . ."

He started the tractor. "Weather report says there's a storm front coming in tonight. If I don't get the hay in, I'll lose it."

"But Grampa, you promised!"

"I'm sorry, Luke. But I've got to get the hay up before the thunderstorms hit. I'll take you next time."

He started the tractor and drove off to the field. My teeth clamped together as I glared after him. "But you promised . . ."

Mama had a coffee break at work around ten. I called and practically begged her to come home and drive me to town. She said she couldn't because this was the day they were supposed to tell her whether she was going to get to work on a permanent basis or not, and she just couldn't ask for time off. Not today.

She did say that I might ask Mike if he'd take me.

I couldn't get him on the phone, so I walked over to his place, only when I got there, his truck was gone and he was nowhere around.

I even tried calling Joshua. He said his mother would come pick me up, but she had gone to Putnam City to visit her sister and wouldn't be back until tonight.

So I was stuck. There was no way to get to town, nothing to do. I just sat around, watching cartoons. Once I thought about going rat hunting in the barn, but Grampa never told me where the shells to the shotgun were because he didn't want me going by myself.

When the cartoons were over at noon, there was nothing but junk on TV. I fixed a batch of chocolate chip cookies, but I only ate a couple of them. I just wasn't that hungry.

Finally, I went to the barn. I messed around there awhile but really couldn't find anything interesting to do, so I went to doctor Beauty's leg.

"Grampa doesn't keep promises any better than Daddy did," I told her.

I put the medicine away and had just closed the gate when Mama drove up. She got out. I waved.

"I'm over here," I called to her.

She opened the back door and held up a grocery sack. "You and your grampa had dinner?"

I shook my head. "He's been in the hayfield all day. Haven't eaten a thing."

"Good," she called back. "I don't mean good that you haven't eaten. I mean good because you're hungry." She tucked the sack under her arm. "I'll put the steaks on for you and your grampa. I got the job. I go to work as a *real* employee, starting Monday. We're gonna celebrate."

"I thought you had a date tonight."

Mama nodded. "I do. Mike and I are going out to celebrate. You and your grampa are having steak. Isn't it great. A real job . . . finally!"

She'd just started for the house when I heard a rattling sound and the roar of an engine. I stopped in my tracks and turned to look.

Mike's truck came flying over the cattle guard at the end of our driveway. He came tearing up the road, fast as he could go. The red dust billowed up in a huge cloud behind him.

He slid to a stop, just inches from the back end of Mama's car. He leaped out and raced around the front of his truck to where Mama was. He was breathing hard. Beads of sweat popped out on his forehead and trickled off the tip of his beard.

He took a deep breath.

"Carol, your daddy's had an accident." He waved

his hands quickly. "He'll be all right. But I think you better come."

He flung open the door to his truck. Mama dropped the grocery sack and jumped in. I started to hop into the back of the truck, only Mike caught me.

"Luke. I've called an ambulance. Do you know how to get to the hayfield?"

I nodded.

"Okay. Wait here by the house. When they get here, get in and show them the way."

I could feel myself shaking all over. I couldn't talk. All I could do was nod my head.

Mike patted my shoulder. "He's hurt, but he's gonna be okay. Understand?"

I nodded.

He jumped in the truck and drove off toward the field. "Bring 'em out as soon as they get here," he yelled out the window.

It took forever for the ambulance to come.

CHAPTER 19

It took even longer for Mike and the two ambulance men to get Grampa out of the hay baler.

I couldn't quit shaking. My hands trembled, so I laced my fingers and held them tight. Then both hands shook. Mama tried to help the men, but there wasn't much she could do, so she stood beside Grampa and held his hand.

Grampa was sitting up on the front edge of the baler. His leg was down inside and stuck. Every time I tried to get close enough to look or to help, somebody would yell at me to get back.

At first I was terrified, since I thought they didn't want me to see how bad it was. Then I figured it was because I was just in the way.

Grampa was doing fine. He wasn't crying or moaning or anything like that. He was talking—growling and fussing like usual. He sure looked pale, though. Mama helped steady him as she held his hand.

One of the men from the ambulance said: "Pull!"

Grampa braced his hands against the frame of the baler. He groaned and shook his head.

"Still stuck." Then to Mama and me: "Should have known better. Long as I been farming, should have known better. I should have turned the tractor off, unplugged the hydraulic." He shook his head again. "Not me. No sir. Old Willie didn't even have sense enough to take the baler out of gear. Just sticks his foot in there and tries to kick it loose when it got stuck. Just cram my foot down in there and kick."

"Try it now," Mike groaned.

He had both arms around a big steel plate, near where Grampa's foot was. He was pulling so hard, his face was turning a bright red. I could see the sweat pop out on his forehead and the big blue veins stand out along the side of his neck.

The two ambulance men pulled. Grampa's leg came free.

"Got him?" Mike groaned.

"He's clear," one of the men answered.

Mike let go of the plate he was holding. There was

a loud banging sound as it flew across the baler and slammed into the other side.

The two men lifted Grampa down off the machine and laid him on the stretcher. One told his friend to get an I.V. started while he took a look at the leg. The man went to the ambulance. He got a bottle with a tube on it. Then he stuck a needle on the end of the tube into Grampa's arm, taped it down, and started the stuff in the bottle dripping.

While he was doing that, the guy on the ground took a pair of scissors and cut off the leg of Grampa's jeans. The leg looked really blue. It was bent over to the side, down below where Grampa's knee was.

"Looks like a clean break," the man said. Then to Grampa, "How long were you in there?"

Grampa shook his head.

"Not very long. Maybe thirty minutes. Mike here—" He motioned. "He was riding that little white filly of his over in his east pasture. Heard me yelling. If it hadn't been for him . . ."

He looked back at the baler when they picked him up and started toward the ambulance.

"Darned thing tried to eat my leg. Should have known better. Jammed, and I go and stick my foot in it while the thing's still running. Dumb . . . stupid."

They loaded him into the ambulance. One man got in with him, and the other got in the front. They wouldn't let Mama ride, so the three of us jumped in Mike's truck and followed Grampa to the hospital.

When we got to the emergency room, Mama was allowed to go with Grampa to see the doctor, but Mike and I had to stay in a little room. There was a TV, an ashtray, and some plastic chairs, but that was all. Mama came to sit with us when they took Grampa to the X-ray room, since they wouldn't let her back there.

It was after dark before the doctor finally came out. He looked at us and walked over to Mike.

"You Willie's son?"

Mike shook his head.

"Just a neighbor."

The doctor turned to Mama. "Your dad's going to be fine," he said with a smile. "He does have a fracture. The bone is broken about six inches below the knee, but it's what we call a 'simple' break. No bone fragments or extensive tissue damage."

I moved closer so I could hear. Mama reached back and patted my arm. I could hear her sigh.

"There is some swelling already. The foot is larger than it should be. I can't tell whether it's from the break or because the circulation was cut off because of the way his leg was pressed in there."

He looked past Mama at Mike.

"You the one who found him?"

Mike nodded and stepped up beside us. The doctor reached out and shook his hand.

"Glad you found him when you did. If he'd stayed in that machinery very long, we might have lost the leg. I'm pretty sure the blood flow was cut off. But thanks to your quick work, we don't have much danger of gangrene."

Mama wrapped her arm around Mike's. She leaned her head against his shoulder.

"He's in excellent condition for a man his age," the doctor went on. "It's going to take a couple of days before we can put a cast on the leg. The swelling has to go down first. I imagine by Wednesday I can put a walking cast on, and we can send him home."

"That's wonderful," Mama said. She squeezed Mike's arm and squeezed mine too. "Can we see him?"

The doctor nodded. "Nurse should have him settled in a room by now. Ask at the second floor desk. Oh, one other thing. Is he really serious about walking out of the hospital if we don't let him smoke his pipe?"

Mama looked at me. I looked at Mama. Then both of us looked at the doctor and nodded.

The doctor smiled. "That's what I figured. I'll leave word that he has permission to smoke his pipe. Otherwise, he probably *will* try to walk out of here and we'll end up having to reset the leg. You can go on up, but I've given him something for the pain, so probably all he'll do is sleep. My advice is to go see him, so you'll know he's all right. Then go home and get some rest. He'll be more in the mood for visiting tomorrow."

We took the doctor's advice. Grampa was sleeping. He opened his eyes, mumbled something when we walked in, said "Hi" to us, and fell back to sleep. We stayed for a while and then went home to rest. Only we didn't rest.

Mike said he needed to get Grampa's hay up in the barn. Mama and I both said we'd help.

We stopped at Mike's house and got his tractor and baler. Then he hooked this thing called a loader up to the side of a big flatbed truck. Mama and I drove the truck and Mike took the tractor.

There were about five rows of hay that Grampa hadn't gotten to. Mike called them windrows. It was where the hay was raked up and ready for the baler. I smiled, finally understanding what a windrow was. Mama and I sat on Mike's truck and waited for him to finish baling the hay. It was a cool night. The wind was blowing, so the mosquitoes weren't bad.

I couldn't help thinking how bright and clear the sky was, how fresh the new hay smelled, and how lucky we were that Grampa was going to be okay.

When Mike was done with the baling, he parked his tractor behind where Grampa's was and walked over to us.

"Luke and I will stack if you'll drive the truck, Carol. What you need to do is bring the front left wheel of the truck as close to the bales as you can. That way they'll hit the loader and it will—"

Mama's voice was both kind of gruff and kind of teasing when she cut him off. "Mr. Garrison, I haven't lived in the city all my life. I *do* know how to drive a hay truck. All you need to do is yell if I get going too fast for you to keep up."

Mike seemed to take that as a dare. With his thumb, he motioned me to get on the truck. Then he jumped up too.

"I think we can keep up."

Mama cocked an eyebrow. Then she jumped in the truck and took off. She didn't drive too fast, but I had to hang onto the wood rails at the front of the truck to keep from being slung all over the flatbed. She drove so the brackets on the loader would hit the hay bales. The flat metal runners kind of scooped them up, then the metal teeth on both sides lifted the bale and dropped it on the truck. I stood and watched Mike stack the first few bales as they landed on the flatbed. Then I started helping, too.

I wasn't all that much help. Mike could grab them

one or two at a time. He'd latch onto the wires and sling them right where he wanted. I had to groan and struggle every time I picked one up. Sometimes it went where I wanted it to, and other times it didn't. I even dropped a couple of bales, accidentally, off the far side of the truck, and Mama had to drive back around to pick them up.

When the truck was loaded, Mike yelled for Mama to stop.

"Getting ahead of you?" she teased.

Mike climbed down.

"Nope. Truck's full. Let me unhook the loader and we'll put this in the barn."

All three of us stacked the hay. I was surprised how much of the hay Mama moved. She was little, but she was pretty strong when it came to tossing hay off the truck or dragging it to where it needed stacking in the barn.

I told Mike to leave a space between the grain bin and Beauty's feed sacks, since that was where Grampa and I hunted rats. In no time at all we had the truck unloaded and were headed back for the next load.

We were just about done with the last load when I noticed the lightning in the west. It was still far far away, because I couldn't hear any thunder. But the storm Grampa had said was coming was really here.

It was good that Mike decided to get the hay up.

When we finished emptying the last truckload, we went to the house. Mama said it was after five in the morning and asked if anybody wanted breakfast. Mike and I both yelled, “Yes!” without even having to think about it.

While Mama was fixing breakfast, I sat down on the couch. Then, when my head started nodding, I thought how nice it would be just to lie down for a minute or two. After that I don’t remember much.

I remember smelling bacon. I remember Mama and Mike talking. I remember opening my eyes when somebody picked me up and carried me to my bed. I remember hearing Mike say something about going home to get cleaned up, then coming back. And mostly I remember how tired my arms were and how good it felt to keep my eyes closed and how clean and crisp and soft the sheets felt.

That’s about all I remember.

CHAPTER 20

I don't know what woke me. I yawned and stretched, blinking the grit out of my eyes. I looked around.

A loud crack of thunder shook my windows. I sat straight up.

It was light outside, but it was dark too. I swung my feet over the side of the bed and rubbed my fingers through my hair. The thunder cracked again. Better check this out, I thought. I staggered to the window and pulled back the curtains.

Outside, the rain was pouring down. It was so thick, I could barely see the barn. The trees swayed, their limbs twisting this way and that way with the roar of the fierce wind. Some of the smaller trees seemed to lie over on their sides.

I closed the window. Somebody had taken my jeans and shirt off, so I found clean clothes and put them on. Then I headed for the kitchen.

"Mama?" I called.

No answer.

"Mike?"

Still nothing.

The kitchen was empty. So was the living room. But there was a note taped to the front door. I yawned and rubbed my eyes again so I could read it:

> Luke,
> Mike and I went to see your grampa. You were sleeping so soundly, we didn't have the heart to wake you. Breakfast is in the oven. If we're not back and you need anything call 555–2300 and ask for room 218.
>
> Love,
> Mama

The rain pounded the roof, but above the sound I could hear my bare feet plopping across the tile floor. The clock on the oven said 12:40. I shook my head.

"Can't believe I slept so late. It's past noon."

I got the food out and started eating. Probably need to go doctor Beauty, I thought. Then, as I glanced out the window and saw the rain pouring down, I figured it could wait.

Instead, I decided to call and check on Grampa. Mama answered the phone in his room. She told me that after she and Mike put me to bed, they ate breakfast. Then Mike went home and got cleaned up, and she took a bath. They came in to see Grampa about eight and had been with him ever since. She said they were going to get lunch and if there was anything I needed from town to let her know.

I talked to Grampa a minute. He was sounding just like he usually did. His voice was gravelly, and he was grumping about the doctors and nurses. That meant he was doing fine. Then, when he finished fussing, he let me talk to Mama again. She said she'd be home in a couple of hours and would drop back to check on Grampa before she left town.

There was a really loud clap of thunder. Right as it cracked, there was a quick but very shrill squeak over the phone.

"That was close," Mama said. "Better get off the phone. Oh, Luke . . ."

"Yes?"

"Is it pretty bad out there?"

I glanced at the window. "Lots of rain and some wind."

Mama sighed. "Well, if it gets too bad, you get in the bathroom in the middle of the house and sit in the tub. Grampa never built a storm cellar, but that middle bathroom is the safest place."

A sound came over the phone, like bacon sizzling in a pan. Outside, the thunder cracked again.

"Love you," Mama said. "I'll call when we start home. 'Bye."

"Love you too, Mama. 'Bye-bye."

I hung up the phone and went back to finish my breakfast. The food was a little cold, but I was really hungry, so I gobbled it down.

A loud clattering sound started about the time I finished my eggs. I glanced up. The sound was coming from the roof. Within seconds, it sounded more like a pounding roar than a clatter.

Glancing out the front window, I could see the little pellets of hail streaking down. I stuffed some sausage in my mouth and went to the door.

With the door open I could see the ice pellets hitting the porch and lawn. The hail was about the size of small English peas. It bounced and scattered, this way and that, as it hit. Within just a few minutes the ground was almost covered.

Then some big chunks of round ice fell. A couple were almost the size of golf balls. And just as quickly as the hail had started, it stopped. Nothing was left but the driving rain.

I slipped out the door. The porch felt cold on my bare feet. When I stepped onto the lawn, the hail made it feel like I was walking on ice, which I was.

Gathering up some of the bigger chunks, I headed back to put them in the freezer to show Mama when she got home.

That's when I saw it!

Through the thick rain I couldn't tell what it was at first. A shape. A form.

It moved through the rain in the distance. A white shape. Almost like a white shadow against the white ground and rain.

A horse.

It moved down the driveway. It was heading for the road.

At first it didn't register, it didn't get through my head what it was, what was happening.

I took my handful of hailstones and went inside. I looked at the little round icy balls as I walked toward the kitchen. I opened the door to the freezer, thinking about the shape I'd seen moving down the road through the rain.

My voice was a whisper—almost so soft I couldn't hear it, a breath of air that slipped through my lips like a soft breeze stirring a cottonwood leaf: "Beauty."

My eyes flashed. The hailstones slipped from my hand and clattered to the tile floor. I turned toward the door. My voice, my soft whisper, was now a scream:

"Beauty!"

The screen ripped when my hands slammed into it to force the door open. Barefoot, I raced into the front yard.

The rain was lighter now. I could see the driveway. I could see my white horse trotting down the road.

I raced after her. I ran harder than I'd ever run in my life.

"Stop, Beauty!" I screamed. "Beauty! Stop!! Come back!"

I didn't feel the icy hail on my bare feet or the steel barb from the barbed wire fence rip through my jeans and tear my leg. I didn't feel the cold rain soaking my shirt.

All I did was run as hard and fast as I could.

"Beauty! Stop! The cattle guard. Come back!"

I fell, scrambled to my feet, and ran even harder than before.

CHAPTER 21

Beauty's scream was like no sound I'd ever heard. It was a haunting, piercing sound. A sound whose pain cut through the pouring rain. A sound whose pain cut through my wet clothes. A sound whose pain cut clear through my insides, and lodged itself in my heart.

I froze in my tracks. I was too late.

Her scream came again.

Clawing and shoving, I fought my way through the tall Johnson grass beside the cattle guard. When I stepped onto the road, the sight before me made me stop and want to run back to the house.

I felt sick inside. My stomach was going to roll over and come out my throat. Beauty was in the cattle guard. Her front feet were buried, past the knees, in the gap between some of the rungs of steel.

I shuddered. "Don't move," I breathed. "I'll help you. Don't move."

It was a useless thing to say. Beauty was jerking and leaping, this way and that. She tried to rear up and pull herself out. And each time she moved and tried to go forward or jerk back, that awful, terrible scream pierced the air.

I ran to her and tried to make her stop.

She kept jerking and screaming.

I ran around in front of her. I grabbed hold of her neck and lifted with every ounce of strength I had.

Nothing happened.

She slung her head, trying to get free. The side of her cheek knocked against my chest and threw me to the ground. I slipped into the cattle guard. One of my legs fell between the bars. I pulled it out.

Quickly, I crawled back to her and shoved her neck, trying to help her get free.

Again, her jerking and flailing around knocked me to the ground. This time my forehead dug into the gravel beside the cattle guard. I scrambled back to my knees.

"I can't," I cried. "I'm not strong enough. I can't get you out."

She screamed again. I tasted blood that the rain

washed from the gash on my forehead. I stood up and wrapped my arms around her neck. I pushed my heels against one of the metal bars on the cattle guard and pulled with all my might.

I couldn't lift her out.

From where I stood, above and beside her, I could see down into the cattle guard.

Her legs were broken. Both turned sideways, below her knees. I could see the bone, sticking through her flesh on the right leg. The blood was already turning her beautiful white hair red.

I pulled again.

She had quit struggling to get out of the cursed thing there on the road. I pulled as hard as I could.

Then . . .

Then we both knew it was too late. I couldn't get her out. And even if I could, it was too late. I let go of her neck, wiping the blood from my eye so I could see.

I could hear her crying, a low, mournful cry that came from somewhere deep within her throat. It was not a scream like I'd heard before, but a cry—like that of a lost child.

I wiped the tears from my eyes. "I'll get help, Beauty. I'll be right back. I promise. I won't leave you long."

I raced for the house. The screen bounced against

the side of the wall, then slammed shut as I charged through it. The blood tasted bitter in the corner of my mouth. I wiped the rain from my eyes and dialed the number Mama had left for me.

Grampa answered.

"I got to talk to Mike," I almost screamed at him. "Hurry. Please!"

"Luke?" Grampa asked. "Is that you? What is it, boy?"

"Grampa," I pleaded, "I got to talk to Mike, please. I need help."

"He's not here, Luke. He and your mom left to get something to eat."

I closed my eyes. I was trembling so much I almost dropped the phone.

"Where is he, Grampa? What's the number? I got to talk to him."

"I don't know where they went. Luke," Grampa said, "You calm down, boy. What's wrong? What is it?"

I sniffed back the tears.

"It's Beauty, Grampa. Beauty . . . she's . . . she's in the cattle guard. She's hurt . . ."

Through my sobs I could hear nothing on the other end of the phone, nothing but a long silence.

"Listen, Luke," Grampa's voice came, finally. "Stay there in the house. Soon as he gets back, I'll get him." He stopped. "No, wait. I'll call the vet. I can find the number."

I had trouble swallowing.

"Where is the vet, Grampa? How far? How long?"

Grampa cleared his throat. "It's on the other side of town from our place, Luke. About an hour. Maybe a little more. You stay in the house. She's caught and trying to get loose and she might accidentally hurt you."

I wiped my face with my sleeve.

"Can the vet do anything, Grampa? Can he help her?"

I heard Grampa sigh. "There's nothing anybody can do, Luke. He can stop the hurting. End her pain. But there's nothing *anybody* can do for a horse . . . not once . . . not . . ."

He stopped talking, and there was nothing but the sound of our breathing over the phone.

"Grampa," I sniffed, finally. "She's hurting, bad. I can't leave her like that. I . . . I got to do something to help her, Grampa. Please . . . she's crying . . . I heard her. Oh, Grampa . . ."

I heard him sniff.

"Luke, there's nothing you can do, boy."

"Grampa, she's hurting . . . something terrible. I got to do something . . . You understand, Grampa, don't you?"

The silence lasted forever.

"Luke?"

"Yes, Grampa?"

"The shells are in the top left-hand drawer of my dresser." Again, there was a long silence. "Don't touch her head with the barrel. Just a few inches away. The spot on her forehead, the spot where her little star is . . . Luke . . ."

"Yes," I gasped.

"Luke . . . I love you."

I hung up the phone. Got the shells out of the drawer. Got the shotgun from the back porch.

The rain poured off my hair in little rivulets across my face. I didn't feel it. I didn't hear the thunder. I didn't feel the gravel under my bare feet.

I simply walked down the road toward my horse. I walked like a dead man, without seeing or hearing anything.

Beauty was no longer struggling when I got there. She looked up at me with her big, brown, sleepy eyes. Those sad, sad eyes.

I reached down, one last time, and scratched her behind the ears, like she loved for me to do.

Then I stepped back and cocked the big shotgun. She watched me with those sad eyes. I aimed at the pretty little star.

And I killed my horse.

CHAPTER 22

Mama and Mike found me lying on the cattle guard with my arms around Beauty's neck. I never told them about crying or praying the Lord's Prayer. I never told them about asking God if someday—long, long from now, when I died—He'd let there be a place and a time for Beauty and me to be together again. Maybe there would be a clear blue pool with tall grass on the banks and a mockingbird that called from a big tree.

You just don't tell anybody things like that, not even your mom.

They took me to the house, but I don't even remember walking back up the road. I don't remember Mama drying my hair or putting dry clothes on me. I do remember when she rubbed the alcohol on the gash at the side of my head because it hurt and made me jump.

Mike was outside. He came in about the time Mama finished doctoring me.

"Come with me," he told us. "I've got something to show you."

We followed him out to Beauty's corral. He showed me the gate. It was locked. Then we walked around to the side where the big cottonwood tree was. A huge limb had broken off during the storm. It had fallen across the wood fence and broken a whole section out.

"Just wanted you to know you hadn't left the gate open. It was shut. This is where she got out."

I looked at it and nodded. I was glad to know I hadn't forgotten to shut the gate. It didn't help my hurting inside, though. It seemed like nothing would ever help that.

We went back to the house. Mama tried to talk to me. I sat and listened to her. But it was like I couldn't hear. I stared out the window. I nodded when I heard her say things. But I really didn't listen. Mike talked to me awhile, too.

He said he'd been around horses for a long, long time. He said he'd never had to do something like that. He said he knew how it must hurt and what a brave and unselfish thing it was that I did.

Only, I knew he really didn't know. Nobody knew the hurt I had inside. Nobody except maybe Grampa.

It was late that evening when we went to see Grampa. He asked Mama and Mike to leave us. He waited until they closed the door, then he held out his arms to me.

I climbed up on his bed. We held each other and cried and cried. We didn't say a thing. We didn't need to.

After a while Mama and Mike came back. Right as we were leaving, Grampa motioned me back to the side of his bed.

"It hurts," he whispered so only I could hear. "I know the hurt. It won't ever go away, but it does get easier. It takes time, but trust me, it will get easier."

I trusted Grampa, but after a couple of weeks I didn't know whether I should. I couldn't stop hurting, no matter how hard I tried.

When I closed my eyes at night, I could see her looking at me. When it was quiet in the house, I could almost hear her scream. I could almost hear the crying sound. And when I went outside, I always looked toward the corral and then down the long, gravel road toward the cattle guard.

Mama tried to help. She talked to me. She took me

to town to play football with Joshua. She even took me to a place in Oklahoma City called White Water, where we spent the day swimming and riding the water slides.

Although Grampa had been home for over a week, we didn't talk much. I guess we both knew it wouldn't do any good. He did hobble out on his crutches one day and fix the corral, where the cottonwood limb had fallen. He had Mike bring Lady over, but I didn't want to ride her.

Grampa didn't try to make me. Instead, he let me be. He fed her and kept her watered.

Mike did all he could, too. One day, right after Grampa got home, I saw him down by the cattle guard with his tractor. He latched a chain onto it and ripped it out of the ground. Then he hooked up a blowtorch to a couple of big bottle things in the back of his truck. He cut that cattle guard into a thousand pieces and threw it onto his flatbed.

The men from the oil company, who Grampa said had put the cattle guard in, drove by once. But they took one look at Mike and didn't even bother to stop and ask what was going on. They just kept driving.

Mike came to the house when he finished filling the hole with gravel. He was shaking. His big, strong, sharp jaw was set far out. "That'll never happen again," he said. Then he went home.

I went back to my room. I sat looking out the window, and when I closed my eyes, I could see that pretty, little star. And I cried.

When school started, Joshua asked me to be on his football team. I told him thanks, but no. I didn't feel much like playing football.

I went to classes, like I was supposed to. I answered when the teachers asked questions. I played at recess and talked in the lunchroom and laughed when all the other guys did. Only, my insides still felt empty.

At home Grampa tried to get me to ride Lady a couple more times. I did once, but it wasn't any fun. Finally, he had Mike come and take her back to his place.

Mama and Mike went out a few times. Grampa got around just about like normal on his walking cast. It had a little rubber knob on the bottom of it, and with the crutch Mama got him, he could do about anything he used to do.

I helped with the dishes and listened to Grampa's stories, and when Mama asked if I liked Mike, I told her yes, since I really did. But at night, when it was time for bed, I tried to find reasons to stay up and watch TV or do my homework or read.

It hurt to close my eyes. It hurt because when I

did, I could see my horse and I felt empty. And I knew that even though Grampa told me it would take time, the empty feeling and the hurt would never go away.

The second Saturday in October we all took Grampa to the doctor to get the cast off his leg. When we got through in town, Mike asked us over to have cake and ice cream.

When we finished eating, I asked if I could go out and walk around. I didn't feel much like getting in on the conversation. I just wanted to be alone, as usual. They seemed a little disappointed, but they let me go.

I found Lady in one of the corrals. I petted her and prowled around some more.

The little white filly was in her pen. I watched her a minute. She ate her oats, came over and looked at me, then walked over by the gate. She turned around and backed up to the big post.

And right there in front of me, she started scratching her bottom. She pushed her hind end way out and rubbed it back and forth on that post. And while she scratched her seat, I could see that goofy look on her face, just like Beauty used to get. I could see her bottom lip flopping up and down, like she was muttering something to herself. She reminded me so much of Beauty, I could hardly stand it.

All of a sudden I heard a laugh. At first it startled me. Then I realized the laugh came from me.

"If you ain't the silliest-looking thing I ever saw," I told her.

Then I laughed and I cried and I did both together, at the same time.

How long I stood there I don't know. Then there was an arm around my shoulder. I kind of jumped and looked up. Mike looked down at me with those soft blue-gray eyes. He didn't say anything, just hugged me. His was the softest, most gentle hug I ever had.

"She's a lot like her grandmother," he said. "She's gentle. She likes to scratch her bottom on posts and . . ." He held me back at arm's length and looked me straight in the eye. "And she likes her ears scratched, too. She's yours if you want her."

Right about then the little filly came over to the fence where I was standing. She leaned down and nudged me with her nose. I reached behind her ears and started scratching.

For the first time in a long, long while, my insides felt almost alive again.

"I'll take good care of her," I promised.

A broad smile came to Mike's face. "I know."

* * *

I bolted for the door. Mama looked up from the dishes.

"Where you going?"

"Ride my horse awhile," I answered.

"Be back before dark. Mike's taking us to the show tonight, remember?"

"I will."

I tore out the door. Grampa was coming up the steps. I almost knocked him down.

"Off riding again?" he asked.

I nodded. He looked past me, making sure Mama was far enough away so she couldn't hear.

"Be sure and put the alcohol and peroxide in your ears when you get back."

I grinned and winked at him. "I will," I whispered.

October in Oklahoma is just downright too cold for swimming. I splashed around in the pool anyway. Dandy—that's what I named the filly—came in too. She splashed the water with her hoof. I splashed her back. Then she went to graze some more on the bank.

It didn't take long for my teeth to start clattering together. I got out, got dressed, and put the saddle on her. We headed back to the house, back to Mama and Grampa and Mike, who'd been coming over almost every evening lately.

"I think he and Mama are getting serious about each other," I told Dandy.

She just wiggled her ears at me.

It was a beautiful afternoon. The birds were singing. The sky was clear and the October air fresh and cool. And I was riding.

It wasn't the Morning Trail.

It was more. Much, much more.

About the Author

Since BILL WALLACE's best-selling first novel, *A Dog Called Kitty,* was published in 1980, he has won nineteen state awards for his children's books.

After seven years as a classroom teacher and ten years as the principal and physical education teacher at West Elementary School, which he attended as a child, Wallace is now a full-time author and public speaker. Bill says that although it has been a while since he taught school, he still writes books for his fourth graders—"It's like they're in my head and heart whenever I sit down to work on a story."

He received his M.S. in Elementary Administration from Southwestern State University and studied professional writing with William Foster-Harris and Dwight V. Swain at the University of Oklahoma.

Literature Circle Questions

Use these questions and the activities that follow to get more out of the experience of reading *Beauty* by Bill Wallace.

1. How does Luke's mother greet Mike Garrison when they first meet? What is Mike's response?

2. Describe Grampa's method for killing rats in the barn. Why does he do it this way?

3. What happens to Beauty when Luke and Joshua play cowboys with Grampa's cattle? How does Grampa react?

4. Luke's mother knew moving in with Grampa wouldn't be easy, but she told Luke she didn't know what else to do. Summarize the circumstances that forced Luke and his mom to move to Oklahoma.

5. Luke finds out quickly that Lady is not at all like Beauty. In your own words, describe how the two horses differ.

6. Promises play an important role in this book. Explain why Luke is surprised when Mike keeps his promise to give him a riding lesson "anytime." Use what you know about Luke's past to support your answer.

7. The characters in the book — human and animal — span three generations. How does the expression "history repeats itself" apply to the oldest and youngest generations in this story?

8. On page 123, Grampa tells Luke's mother that "if you're too scared to trust or to love, you might as well quit living altogether. You can't go through this world without trusting or loving. That ain't living." How could Luke also benefit from this advice?

9. When Luke first meets his grandfather, he describes him as "mean and cruel and heartless" (p. 36). As they get to know each other, Luke begins to see Grampa's softer side. List at least three situations in which Luke discovers what's behind Grampa's gruff exterior.

10. At the beginning of the novel, the way Luke remembers his experiences with his father on the Morning Trail is better than they actually were. Even after he learns to ride Beauty, Luke says he thinks he likes "Colorado riding" better than "Oklahoma-type riding" (p. 65). How has Luke's view of the Morning Trail changed by the story's end?

11. Imagine that Luke has decided to write his father a letter to confront him about his broken promises and to tell him about his new life in Oklahoma. What do you think he would say? Compose the letter, incorporating Luke's feelings about his parents' divorce and details about how Luke has been spending his time.

12. When Luke and Joshua go out riding together, Joshua persuades Luke to disobey his grandfather's orders and run the cows. What is your opinion of Joshua? If you were Luke, would you have been so easily convinced? If not, how would you have handled the situation differently?

13. Though Luke's relationship with his father is troubled, Luke is able to develop positive relationships with Grampa and Mike. In your view, what makes an adult a good role model? Evaluate Luke's father, Grampa, and Mike based on your criteria.

14. Luke is miserable when he arrives in Oklahoma, but by the end of the book, he has become comfortable in his new surroundings. Which character do you think did the most to help Luke adjust to Oklahoma — Grampa, Mike, Joshua, Beauty, or Dandy? Use details from the text to support your answer.

Note: These questions are keyed to Bloom's Taxonomy *as follows: Knowledge: 1–3; Comprehension: 4–6; Application: 7–8; Analysis: 9–10; Synthesis: 11; Evaluation: 12–14.*

Activities

1. The novel includes many terms used by people who own and ride horses. Create an illustrated glossary of horse-related terms. Include definitions for the words *rodeo, colt, filly, corral, saddle, mare, trot, gallop, stirrup, bridle,* and *halter*.

2. Horses play central roles in many legends, films, and works of literature, from *Black Beauty* to *The Horse Whisperer*. Choose a myth, book, or movie about another fictional horse to read or watch. Then write a report that compares and contrasts that horse with Beauty.

3. Humans have had close relationships with horses for thousands of years. Use the Internet or other resources at a local library to research the history of horses. Prepare a presentation for your class about what you have learned.

4. Mike Garrison's riding class helps Luke meet new people and become more comfortable handling horses. Create an advertisement for the riding class that might persuade a nervous person to give the lessons a try.

Other Books by this Author

A Dog Called Kitty; Trapped in Death Cave; Ferret in the Bedroom, Lizards in the Fridge; Red Dog; Snot Stew; The Christmas Spurs; Totally Disgusting!; The Biggest Klutz in Fifth Grade; Coyote Autumn; Goosed; Skinny-Dipping at Monster Lake; No Dogs Allowed!; Pick of the Litter; The Dog Who Thought He Was Santa

Author's Web site: http://www.wallacebooks.com